# GAME OF GARLANDS

# GAME OF GARLANDS

FRANK MORIN

Whipsaw Press

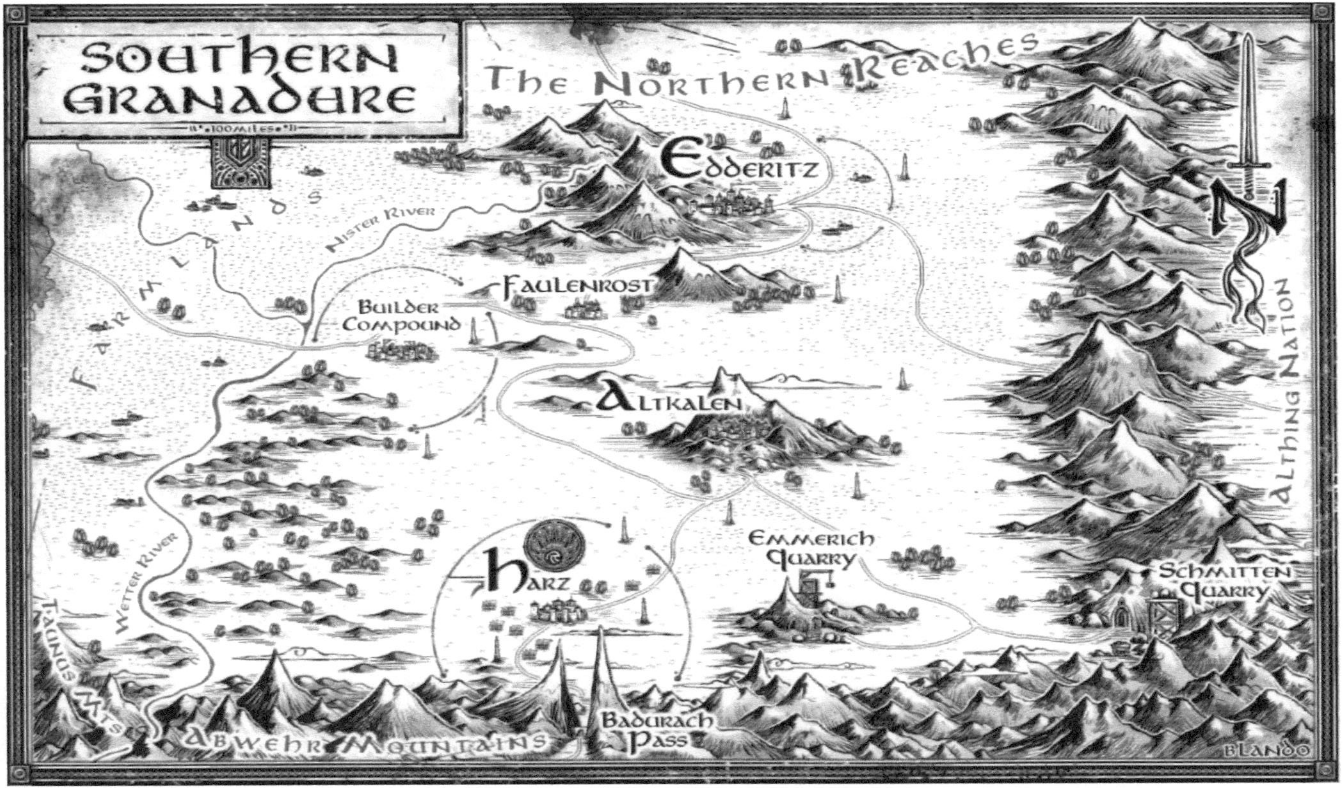

SOUTHERN GRANADURE
11°·100 MILES·11
The Northern Reaches
Edderitz
Farmlands
Nister River
Faulenrost
Builder Compound
Altkalen
Althing Nation
Emmerich Quarry
Harz
Schmitten Quarry
Wetter River
Taunus Mts
Abwehr Mountains
Badurach Pass
BLANDO

The Northern Reaches
Varvakis
Orlov
Platov
River Angara
Lake Pyasino
Krashnov
River Olenet
Althing
Valeska Rivers
Granadure
Jagdish
Ravinder
Edduritz
Dagmanson
R. Anok
Finnlaugur
River Sanjit
Prahalad
R. Baol
R. Bergrin
Obrion
R. Macantacht
Donleavy
The Broken Water
Maninder
The Western Sea
The Eastern Sea
Sea of Olcan
N
Behrad
Ozlem
Hayreddin
Murex
Tabnit
Mahzun
Tabnit
The Known World

# FLOWERS REALLY ARE THE KEY TO A HEART'S DESIRE

Anika ducked, and her brother's rock-hard fist passed so close to her face she could have bit it. He grabbed for her hair, but she flicked it away before he could grab it.

"Nice try, Erich," she teased as she slammed her knuckles into his ribs. She hadn't let him fling her into the wall by the braid in weeks.

Even though neither of them wore battle leathers while practicing in the stone-walled patio behind their parents' home, Erich didn't flinch at her punch. Striking his granite-hardened, blue-tinged torso felt like punching a living wall, but it was so much more fun. Anika's heart raced with the thrill of the fight, and all her senses felt more alive when she was tapping granite and immersed in battle, even if it was only a friendly bash fight with her older brother.

Erich caught her in the side of the head with his return back fist. It felt like getting hit by a tree, and the impact knocked her to the hard-packed earth. She rolled and returned to her feet, crouched and ready for his next blow.

Instead he paused and said, "Good move. If I hadn't

increased my tap rate at the last second, you would've cracked a rib."

She returned his grin. She loved the unrivaled feeling of granite power that hardened her muscles and transformed her into a perfectly-sculpted living statue. She was the best battle maiden in her company, and she'd never backed down from any challenger.

Erich just happened to be a little older, a little more experienced, and probably fifty pounds of hard muscle heavier. That gave him an advantage that she was still trying to overcome. She loved the challenge, and loved that she could train so hard with him.

The early morning air in the practice yard was cool, carrying the scents of earth and stone, overlaid by the smell of mother's cooking. Those tantalizing smells wafted out of the open dining room window that looked out over the practice yard.

Anika raised her fists and said, "I haven't broken one of your ribs in a month. Let me try that again."

His grin faded and his tone turned warning. "You can't be asking for permission around Captain Ilse. Any sign of weakness, and you'll fail to make the team. You'll have a hard enough time as it is."

"That was just a turn of phrase," she objected.

"Turn it a different way next time."

"Krokus," she cursed softly to herself. She wasn't about to let him see how much the looming test worried her. She couldn't imagine not making the elite team. "You made it. How hard can it be?"

He chuckled and released granite. His skin, which had looked mottled blue while tapping his affinity, returned to normal. The Clemens granite that Erich preferred provided exceptional power, but tended to run out faster than other strains of power stone. Erich didn't often worry about it.

He usually beat down any opponents so fast that the quicker exhaustion time didn't matter.

Anika preferred stone from the Walther quarry in the eastern mountains. The delicate, rose-tinted stone produced a steady, dependable strength, and it tinted her skin that same rose hue. A girl could feel pretty even when engaged in mortal combat.

Erich said, "I don't have time to stand around chatting all morning. I've got extra duty today. I'll show you why I made it."

Thorn and blossoms, she needed to return to the barracks early too. If only the extra shifts were for combat duty. She'd love that. Unfortunately, the prince's upcoming international summit was filling everyone's schedule with mundane drivel. She hadn't gotten to punch anyone outside of training in eleven days. And everyone was so busy, she hadn't gotten even a halfway decent wrestling proposal in even longer.

She hoped the actual delegates from all the nations of the Arishat League proved more interesting. If not, the whole political mess meant sausage to her. Still, time was short, so she had to beat Erich now.

Her brother tapped granite again. His skin shifted to blue and his already well-developed muscles swelled and hardened. He charged, but Anika was ready. She slipped around his first couple of punches, focusing on not getting hit and on figuring out something different to finally beat him.

They'd been sparring for over five minutes, and although she was faster than Erich, she couldn't always avoid his hammer-like blows. She had to max-tap granite most of the bout. That vastly increased her strength and the protection of her hardened skin, but also burned much faster through the powdered granite she'd absorbed through her skin to fuel her affinity. That meant she might run out first, even though he was using Clemens stone.

Running out of granite was an embarrassing way to end a friendly bash fight, but it happened all too often. She promised herself today would be different. Today needed to be different.

So when he again snapped fists toward her face, she ducked to the left. Instead of throwing another jab that would ultimately do nothing to slow him, she side-kicked his leading foot, just before he took his next step.

Erich stumbled.

Anika grabbed his right arm and, using it as a lever, flung her legs up and wrapped them around his neck, locking her ankles behind. Continuing the motion, she swung her entire body sideways, dragging him off his feet.

They struck the ground hard and she rolled away, laughing. Max-tapping granite, Erich could rip full grown trees out of the ground, but he still could fall if his balance wasn't set properly.

By the time he staggered back to his feet, muttering a curse about annoying little sisters, she had already grabbed an eight-foot log, almost three feet in diameter. She smashed him in the face with it. The heavy log splintered against his rock-hard skull, and the blow again threw him from his feet.

The back door of the house opened to her right. Their father peeked out and scowled at the cracked and splintered wood. "Don't just stand there, girl. Hit him again. Try to break the wood off more evenly this time. When you're finished, come in for breakfast."

"Yes, Father."

Anika charged Erich as he stood, aiming another heavy blow at his face. They had already splintered most of the wood their parents would need to fuel the winter fires, but father constantly complained that they didn't break it into regular lengths. The uneven, jagged sections were hard to stack.

So she decided to beat Erich with that log until she reduced it to kindling. Erich was ready this time though, and he caught it. As they grappled over the log, Anika max-tapped granite and drew upon every ounce of strength to break it free of Erich's grasp. Her body shifted to perfect lines, every exquisitely-sculpted muscle straining for dominance. She would show him she could match him strength for strength.

Anika growled with the effort as the log began to creak under the strain of their superhuman struggle. Erich's lips pulled back from his teeth in a fierce grin as he bent his strength to beat her.

He max-tapped, and his already bulging muscles grew larger still. She felt the shift through the log and realized she'd already lost half a heartbeat before it happened. With a heave of his massive shoulders, Erich yanked her right off her feet and smashed her into the triple-reinforced concrete wall at the back of the practice yard.

The brutal impact actually rattled her for a second. By the time her vision cleared, Erich stood over her and poked her in the center of the forehead with one thick finger.

"Match."

"Brute," she growled as she accepted his proffered hand and let him haul her back to her feet.

She released granite, and her body returned to normal. Erich sometimes complained that releasing his powers was depressing, but Anika didn't see it that way. She loved her granite-hardened, Rumbler battle body, but she liked being herself too.

At nineteen, she was at the peak of health and fitness. She was tall for a girl, nearly able to look Erich in the eye.

The two of them shared the same shade of blond hair and sparkling blue eyes. She was glad the likeness didn't extend to his big muscles, thick limbs, and wide face. She liked the fact that she wasn't a skinny twig of a woman, but also not built like a tree trunk.

Erich nudged her with a shoulder. "You lose, little sister, so you do dishes."

"Don't rub it in." She glanced at the wall he'd smashed her into. The concrete sported a new crack. She grimaced. "Father won't be happy about that."

Erich grunted. "I say we stack the next pile of wood right there."

"Done." She clapped hands with him and said, "I almost had you that time."

"Never gonna happen, little sister. You're a good fighter, but you'll never out-wrestle me. You need to fight smarter."

"That shouldn't be too hard."

He grabbed for her long braid, but she skipped out of range and led the way inside. After washing the sweat from their hands and faces, they joined their parents at the breakfast table.

"How did it go?" Father asked.

"I almost had him," Anika insisted.

Father asked Erich, "So, is she ready?"

Erich paused before answering, and Anika fought down another flutter of nerves by checking the flowers in the large vase at the center of the table. She'd prepared the arrangement the day before, and the blossoms still looked fresh. The colors were a vibrant mix of delicate, white edelweiss, bright blue cornflowers, and purple crocuses.

Erich said, "I can't think of any other battle maidens who could beat you, but Ilse is looking for more than just fighters."

"What do you mean?" Anika asked with a frown. "She's

assembling an elite team of warriors. How can she do that if she doesn't pick the best fighters?"

The problem was no one knew exactly what Captain Ilse planned to do with her special new team. She was already a star in General Wolfram's staff, and word about a new team had spread through the ranks like wildfire. Ilse and her husband, Lucas, already commanded the Crushers, the most elite force in the entire Grandurian army.

Erich and Anika had both planned to join the Crushers until they heard about the new team. Speculation ran wild about the potential missions Ilse might be assigned, and Anika yearned to take part in them. So far Erich was the only Rumbler to make the team. Anika planned to be the second, but the rather loose requirements made preparations difficult and nerve-wracking.

Mother interrupted her thoughts by placing a huge platter of sausages, eggs, and ham onto the table. She was already dressed for the day, wearing a stylish, if faded, dress under her apron. She'd styled her silvery hair into loose curls, even though she was old enough that she shouldn't still worry about such things. Anika's parents might not be rich, but her mother didn't let that keep her from staying current with fashion trends.

Erich filled his plate to overflowing and began shoveling enormous helpings into his mouth. Anika heaped her plate just as full, but pointed her fork at her brother and said, "What did you mean by that comment?"

He swallowed and she read concern in his eyes. "I hadn't been worried for you. I'm on the team, so I figured you'd get in easy."

"Just because you're on it? Are you suggesting I couldn't do it without your help?"

He raised an eyebrow, as if the point was a given. "You're a great fighter, Anika, but you've followed my every footstep. Do you really think you would've risen through the ranks so quickly and caught Ilse's eye without my influence?"

"Of course." She filled her voice with absolute confidence, but hated that dark little fear that rose to haunt her yet again. She had wondered often about that very point, and as much as she told herself and everyone who brought it up that Erich's assistance didn't mean anything, she had to wonder.

While she worried about Erich's words, she began pulling the flowers out of the vase and weaving them into an intricate crown wreath. She barely looked as she worked, her fingers moving by feel as she added in more flowers and a pattern emerged. The work helped calm her.

Father said between mouthfuls, "Stop worrying, Anika. You'll make the team and make us proud. What does it matter how you get there?"

"It matters that I get there on my own merits."

"That's exactly what you'll have to do, but that's the reason I'm a little worried," Erich said. He lowered his fork. "I've helped you every way I could, but that might actually make things harder for you this time."

"How is that possible?" Father asked.

"Yesterday, Xaver took his test. He failed."

"What?" Anika gasped. Xaver was one of the best fighters in all of Granadure, had come in second behind Erich in the last two annual bash fighting games. She'd figured his acceptance on the new, elite team was all but guaranteed.

Erich shook his head. "Ilse said he was a gifted fighter, and a credit to the prince's guard, but that's not enough to make the team."

"What more could she want?" Father asked. "If Xaver can't make it, who can?"

"Someone with leadership potential, who sees the difference between strategic and tactical situations, and who can think fast and adapt to unexpected situations."

That was a daunting list, and Anika marveled that Erich had passed all those requirements. He was the undisputed champion Rumbler in all of Granadure, but she'd never considered him smart or strategically clever.

Maybe Ilse needed one bash fighter she could simply point in the right direction and unleash overwhelming destruction. Ilse was legendarily clever, so maybe she figured she could do the thinking for Erich. He could out-bash anyone, but for the first time Anika wondered if maybe there were aspects to him that she hadn't noticed in her single-minded drive to perfect her own fighting abilities.

While she considered that, she continued working the crown wreath, shifting the pattern and changing the entire construct into a looping weave, the kind her mother loved to wear across her shoulders in the afternoons while reading.

To conceal her worry, Anika teased, "So how did you make it?"

"I'm on, so I'm not the one who has to worry." Erich fixed her with the most serious expression she'd seen from him maybe ever. "You do. You've always chosen to do exactly what I've done and what I'm best positioned to help you with. You've never proven you can do anything on your own, that you're more than just a talented follower."

"I can't help it if I enjoy doing the same things you do," she exclaimed.

"But not all the same things," Mother pointed out. She had served herself less than a quarter of the helping that Erich and Anika had. Neither of their parents had any Petralist gift, and sometimes it shocked Anika how little they needed to sustain themselves.

"All the things that matter," Anika said.

"But you're not the same person, dear. You're a great fighter, but do we really need two special-forces Rumblers in the family?"

Anika rolled her eyes, and Father grunted, looking disgusted by the suggestion. He loved the honor and prestige that their family won from Erich and Anika doing so well in the armed forces.

Erich laughed. "What else would Anika do?"

"I do other things," she insisted.

"I can't think of one thing you've done on your own," he teased.

"Then you should release granite from your head. You're squeezing what little brains you have left," Anika snapped.

Erich sat back and said, "Fine. Name one thing you would even consider doing as a career that I haven't already done first."

The question caught her by surprise and she hesitated, her fingers stopping work on the nearly-completed flower construct. She really did love fighting with granite strength more than anything, but it wasn't the only thing that defined her, was it?

Erich grunted. "Come on. If you can't convince me, you'll never convince Captain Ilse."

Father said, "Stop worrying so much. You'll make it, or you'll continue with the battle maidens. Either way is honorable. I can't imagine anything better that you should even try."

He was right, but also wrong. She so desperately wanted to make that team. No, by heiderkraut, she needed to make that team. But Erich's question hung in the kitchen, and she hated how long it was taking her to come up with an alternative.

"You love working with flowers," Mother said, pointed to the nearly finished arrangement in her hands, then toward a long wreath chain Anika had hung around the window a few days ago. The daisies were still looking good, but the irises and lavender were starting to droop.

Both Erich and Father burst into laughter, turning Anika's annoyance into anger. Her love of flowers was deep rooted, and she'd thrown more than one battle maiden out a window of their barracks when teased about all the intricate flower arrangements she was constantly creating. Maybe she should be a bit more open to criticism, but her flower art was as much a passion as her love of wrestling.

The laughter from her brother and father sparked that defensive rage she always felt around her delicate blossoms. Anika rose so abruptly that she knocked her chair backward. She pointed an angry finger at Erich. "Fine. I'll prove it to you and Ilse both. I can do anything, and I can do it without your help."

Erich wiped his eyes, his expression incredulous. "You can't be serious. Filling a basket with flowers and selling them on some street corner doesn't prove anything."

"It will if I conquer all other florists and prove I'm the best," Anika retorted, the beginnings of a plan forming in her mind.

"Florist aren't fighters," Mother objected. "You can't go around beating up those poor girls."

Father added, "Don't do anything to embarrass the family."

"I won't beat them up, but by krokus I will beat them," Anika said.

Erich asked, "What are you talking about?"

"The summit. The big summit with the Arishat nations. The prince is holding a floral competition in a few days, and the winner earns the right to oversee decorating the summer palace for the summit."

Erich looked confused, but Mother perked up at the mention of the competition. "Oh, yes. The whole town is buzzing about the floral competition. It'll be a huge event. It'll take up Golm's entire central square. The prince himself will participate in the judging."

"How did you come up with that?" Erich laughed, still looking like he didn't believe her.

"Because I do more than bang my head against stone walls when I'm not on duty." Anika was getting swept up in the thrill of the challenge, envisioning herself single-handedly vanquishing entire cohorts of florists assembled against her.

"You're serious about this?" Erich asked, looking doubtful. "Sure you're amazing at working flowers, but really? A florist?"

Father looked dumbfounded by the idea, and mother looked close to tears. Anika decided they were tears of joy. She could do it, could prove to Erich, Ilse, and more importantly, to herself that she didn't need her big brother smoothing her path for her. She would slay that doubt once and for all, and she would do it through her passion for flowers.

So she leaned over the table and declared, "Absolutely. I will become the champion florist, defeat all the other florists combined, and the prince himself will recognize my abilities. That has to be good enough for Ilse."

## 2

## SOMETIMES INSPIRATION NEEDS AN EMPTY ROOM

Four days later, Anika returned from scouting the florist positions in the city, feeling disgusted by what she'd seen. With battle maiden duty assignments so busy, she'd found little time to prepare her assault on the floral organization. Finally that morning she'd managed to slip away.

When she stepped into her parents' front sitting room, she stopped in surprise. Instead of the cozy, cramped room, overflowing with heavy, wooden furniture in a style that had been popular a generation ago, the room was nearly empty. She hadn't realized it was so big.

Usually the room smelled of wood polish and afternoon tea. Now a slight, cool breeze blew in from the back of the house. "What's going on here?"

Mother appeared from the kitchen and grinned. "Oh my dear, I had hoped to finish before you returned."

"Finish what? Moving out?"

Erich lumbered in behind mother and chuckled, "More like retreating in the face of guaranteed defeat. Trying to salvage a little of the family honor."

"Very funny," Mother chided and gestured toward a large, wooden hutch that usually held her best china. All the dishes had been removed, and it looked somehow forlorn, standing alone in an empty corner of the room. "Take that out with the rest."

Erich barely needed any granite to hoist the heavy piece. He was naturally one of the strongest men Anika had ever met.

"So what are you doing, then?" she asked.

Father stepped into the room, shifted aside for Erich to pass, and called after him, "Careful, Son. I don't want that blocking my chair." He gave Anika a frustrated look. "I hope you're satisfied."

"With what exactly?"

"Crazy ideas have a way of breeding," Father grumbled. "Mother's caught up in the insanity now."

"Oh, hush," Mother chided, and came to Anika, smiling with delight in a way Anika had rarely seen. "He never could deal with changing anything."

"I can too," Father huffed."

"Then stop whining."

"I'm not whining."

"Of course you are, dear. Just remember that you said yourself you'd do anything to help Anika succeed."

"I know what I said, but I never imagined I'd have to move my favorite reading chair to do it."

"Well you can stay out in the shed and read all you like," Mother declared, giving him a warning look.

Still grumbling, father paced around the room, as if visualizing where everything was supposed to be.

"I don't understand," Anika said.

Mother spread her arms wide and said, "You need a place to work, to prepare for the competition. This is the only room big enough for the job."

"Oh." Wow. She hadn't expected the rest of the family to help, and the gesture warmed her heart. She really did need a room big enough to build her display booth and prepare her arrangements. She'd planned to use the training patio, but the weather was threatening rain, and that could wreck everything.

"Thanks," she said, and meant it.

She needed to succeed on her own, but that didn't mean she couldn't let her mother make a little sacrifice too. She seemed so pleased with herself, and father did need to learn to deal with changing things sometimes. Maybe he'd finally get a new reading chair to replace that nasty old one he'd used since she was a little girl.

Erich returned, dusting off his hands. She was surprised he'd found any time off. He was supposed to be on duty. "So, how did your reconnaissance of the competition go, Sis?"

Anika rolled her eyes, her frustration returning instantly. "Florists are basically useless."

"They are not," Mother protested, looking shocked. "Just think of what you can do with all those flowers you've ordered. You might even catch the eye of an eligible young lord or wealthy merchant."

"Mother . . . " Anika warned.

Erich had started drinking from a large tankard of water. He snorted with laughter and squirted water right out his nose. Wiping his face, he said, "You want her to start throwing young lordlings out palace windows? I've never met a nobleman with a fraction of the determination he would need to try to court our Anika."

"You don't have to fight so hard against a man who is clearly eligible," Mother suggested.

Anika wished she'd show a fraction as much interest in getting Erich married off. Mother did not seem to understand the importance of proving herself and winning her dream career before she even considered finding a man strong enough for her to consider surrendering to.

Erich regularly grumbled about how several of his friends secretly wished to court her, but he'd never yet gotten to stand in and defend her honor as a brother. He seemed eager for a chance to beat down any potentially serious suitors.

She'd had dozens of offers, but few men were actually willing to accept her terms. Anika loved wrestling, and had decided several years ago that she would not consider any suitor who could not successfully wrestle with her. She'd easily beaten every suitor who had tried. Most of them hadn't suffered serious injuries, but none of them came back to wrestle again.

She was starting to wonder if she'd ever find a man strong enough and honorable enough to seriously tempt her to surrender.

She hadn't found one yet.

"Leave off, dear. You're going to distract Anika from her mission," Father warned.

"So if you win champion florist, win the patronage of the prince himself, do you think you'll be tempted to set yourself up as a rich florist?" Erich asked with a laugh in his voice.

Using the word patronage was low, even for Erich. Only Obrioners worried about that bizarre practice.

She gave him a disgusted look. "Of course not. I told you, my only interest is proving myself to Captain Ilse."

Mother gave her an encouraging smile. "I bet the competition will be fierce. Don't let the other florists intimidate you during set up. You do beautiful work, dear, but not when you let yourself get distracted."

Erich chuckled. "Don't worry. If anyone gives Anika

trouble, she'll just wrap their flower arrangements around their face and throw them into the river."

Father tried to conceal his laugh behind a hand, but Mother looked appropriately horrified. "Oh, no. You can't start brawling. I'm sure that would be a disqualifying offense."

"There's no one to brawl with anyway," Anika said, thoroughly disgusted by that fact. "That's the problem. There's no organization at all."

She loved flowers, felt absolutely confident that her bouquets and wreaths and arrangements could compete against the best from any florist in their home town of Golm, or even all the way from Edderitz. The problem was not too much competition, but lack thereof.

When she'd started scouting her opposition and analyzing their strengths, she'd been startled to learn how disorganized they were. She'd dreamed of planning a grand incursion against the floral establishment, taking out their leadership in a sweeping campaign of shock and awe that would leave her the undisputed champion.

But she was starting to realize that would never work. Florists lacked a guild, an artisan circle, or any kind of official organization. As she had explored the city and visited nauseating numbers of floral shops and stands and carts, she had grown increasingly disgusted with her choice of profession. It seemed anyone with a basket of flowers could call themselves a florist.

How could she prove herself the best floral battle maid if she had no competition? She could not bring herself to buy a little cart or simply fill a wheelbarrow with flowers, park it on some random street corner, and hawk her wares for whatever pennies the uncaring pedestrians were willing to pay as they hurried past.

On the other hand, if Obrion managed their florists as

poorly as Granadure did, she had identified the perfect cover to infiltrate the enemy if she was ever called upon to do so. The heady scent of beautiful flowers seemed to dull the senses and make even the most astute observer pass by without giving the florist more than a passing glance. That is, except for the men who seemed as eager to flirt with a pretty florist as they were to buy flowers for their sweethearts.

Father said, "Maybe that's a good thing."

"If it's too easy, I won't impress Ilse," Anika explained, voicing her greatest fear.

Erich said, "You've declared an assault. Backing down now would be worse. Just focus on winning the challenge competition. You'll still get to impress the prince."

Mother nodded eagerly, no doubt thinking about all those eligible, useless lords.

Anika rubbed her hands together and surveyed the empty room as she focused her thoughts. She would need a table to begin sketching out her plans. She'd started ordering some flowers, but would need to buy most of her stock in the days leading up to the competition. She was committing all of her savings. She'd accrued a little money from her military pay, above what she sent to her parents to help supplement their meager income.

Erich helped them too. He'd earned a hefty bonus when Ilse accepted him to the new team. The prize money for winning the floral competition could make a huge difference. It was a risk, but one had to commit resources in order to execute a successful campaign.

The first step was to plan everything out. She did worry about preparing her arrangements with the other florists looking on, or even possibly teasing her for being the newest applicant. That would seriously distract her.

Working with flowers fulfilled a need in her heart that

not even bash fighting could fill, and she guarded it jealously. Whenever anyone teased her about the flowers, she easily grew defensive and couldn't continue working until that person left.

If any of the other florists realized that during set-up, she'd be doomed. Failure was not an option, though. Failing to a gaggle of untrained girls would guarantee she'd lose any hope of winning a spot with Captain Ilse. She needed a battle plan, needed some kind of shock and awe campaign to remove any chance they could interfere.

As she turned a slow circle in the empty room, trying to visualize how she would fill it with breathtaking floral arrangements, she realized the simple answer.

No rule stated she had to do all her set-up there in the square. In fact, there was no way she could complete all the work in one morning. No, she would build her entire booth and all of her arrangements before she even left for the competition.

She grinned, surprised to feel a thrill similar to what she felt when stepping onto the dueling court for mock battles.

The other florists were doomed.

## 3

## FULL-CONTACT FLORAL COMPETITION

One week later, Anika arrived at the central square of Golm, mentally prepared to vanquish all other florists in intense floral combat. Instead of a hammer or sword, she wielded her entire flower-filled booth. She'd reluctantly left her leather battle armor behind, choosing instead a deep blue, cotton dress, with a gold satin belt that encircled her narrow waist. The colors enhanced the effect of her rose-tinted, granite hardened skin.

She was ready, although she still would have preferred the prince simply invite all the florists into the palace itself. That would have reduced the number of gawking fools she'd have to deal with.

No such luck.

Anticipation for the summit was rising to a fever pitch, and their small community was inundated with soldiers needed for increased security, an army of officials required to administer the summit, and hordes of merchants hunting lucrative contracts. Golm was only twenty miles from

Edderitz, but despite its location close to the large military complex and the prince's summer palace, it was usually a quiet, uneventful place.

Not today. Anika felt shocked by the sight of so many people. Didn't they have anything better to do than gawk at flowers?

Apparently not. Crowds packed the square, even though the official competition wouldn't start for another couple hours. Most of the other florists had already arrived. Many had probably begun work on their presentations the day before, and might have worked through the night.

The large, cobbled square had never felt too small before. It usually seemed a bit grand for their peaceful town. The plain, four-story government office building lorded over the square on the north end, while the high, gray tower of the judgment hall reared to the south. Some of the most influential shops crowded the western side. The second-story residences above the shops were packed with privileged guests already lounging and eating on small, railed balconies or watching through open windows.

A high-class inn dominated the entire eastern side of the square, with a façade of expensive, non-power-grade granite rising up all three stories. Ornate columns and statues of great Grandurian Petralists added to its grandeur. Many of the retinue of the Arishat delegates would be staying there.

But the pomp and grandeur of those buildings, which usually overshadowed everything else, served only to reinforce the dramatic transformation of the rest of the square. The florists were all set up around the huge fountain at the heart of the square. Each florist was assigned ten feet of space to display their best work, and the concentration of their beautiful arrangements created a riot of vibrant colors.

The growing crowds were already moving in slow rotation around them, like the beginnings of a human whirlpool.

The tall, five-tiered fountain seemed intent on cowing the best attempts of the florists, though. Its waters shot nearly a hundred feet into the air, constantly changing hue through all the colors of the rainbow. That was a nice touch. Anika wondered if the prince had ordered a Solas and a Water Moccasin to put on that display, or if the merchants had funded the idea in hopes of drawing in even bigger crowds and improving sales.

It looked like sales would be exceptional. Already vendors hawked all sorts of wares. The floppy, woolen hats that were the new fashion trend, most dyed in bright reds and blues of the king's colors, were selling well. Dozens of people were also purchasing small Grandurian flags, either to wave their patriotism to the prince when he arrived, or to show any foreigners their national pride.

Delicious smells of dozens of fresh-cooked foods wafted across the square, mixing with the heady perfumes of all of those fresh flowers. Instead of breads and sausages most people enjoyed for breakfast on other days, long lines of eager patrons were buying warm pastries and cakes.

As usual, bethmannchen was a favorite. The soft pastry bread, with marzipan and almonds, sprinkled with sugar, was more often seen in the midwinter festival. Sweet, cinnamon-flavored franzbrotchen was selling just as fast, while colorful, jellied gotterspeise were everywhere.

Anika registered all of that in her initial tactical sweep of the terrain, but saw nothing to make her worry, or consider changing her assault plan. Tapping a bit of granite from her carefully hoarded personal stash, she again hefted her large display platform over her head and marched into the square.

She drew a lot of attention as she moved through the

thick crowds, who melted out of her path. She was pleased to hear quite a few exclamations of wonder at the sight of her creations.

As she approached the presentation area, the nearest florists caught sight of her, and most of them stopped to stare. Anika ignored them, careful to keep her platform balanced. It wasn't really all that heavy, but it liked to tip over. The ten-by-ten foot square booth was built with a light, wooden framework that supported built-in shelves and racks to display her flowers. She'd carefully designed exquisite arrangements, which were secured in wicker crates.

All of that preparation had been pretty straight-forward. The tricky part had been the tall, flowering waterfall feature that she'd needed to fold down across the top of the booth for transport. Figuring out how to build that support structure, but still fold it for travel without damaging the flowers, had kept her up for two straight days.

Now she felt a growing sense of confidence as she carefully carried her booth into position. A space had been left for her, but the two florists on either side had started encroaching into it. They probably figured since she was the last to arrive, she would have less time to prepare her arrangements, and therefore would be too distracted to protest.

Anika put down her platform, walked around it and gave the two gaping florists a hard look. She decided tact might be a good way to begin so instead of simply ripping their flowering vines and potted plants away she said curtly, "You have five seconds to get out of my space."

Then she walked back around to her platform and began pushing it into the opening. The two florists scrambled to move their encroaching arrangements, shouting for her to wait.

She didn't. Even though someone had clearly marked the dimensions of each booth onto the cobblestones with chalk, the two florists had just as clearly ignored those marks. Bad move. Anika had built her platform to exact measurements, and she was not about to cede ground so early in the campaign.

As the other women scrambled to pull their flowers back, Anika managed to knock over one potted plant on the left side and crush the base of an arched, flower-laden trellis on the other. The trellis buckled, sending flowers raining down and blowing across the square in the light breeze. Some of the spectators gasped and pointed, while children scrambled to pluck the free-blowing flowers from the ground.

The florist to Anika's left, a young woman with a pretty face and a festive, colorful dress, scowled at Anika with hands on hips. "What do you think you're doing, you brute? We were already set up here, and you've undone half an hour of work."

She was all bluster, clearly clueless about how to follow up those angry words. The woman on the right, a plump, mature lady looked like she usually liked to smile. At the moment though, she was muttering darkly to herself as she scrambled to fix the broken trellis. She lacked a warrior's heart, so posed no immediate threat either.

Anika ignored them both. She stepped into the booth, took a deep breath to savor the rich scents of her flowers, then grabbed the hoist rope and started to pull. As her flowering waterfall feature rose above her booth, the angry florist fell silent, while many nearby spectators clapped and pointed.

Anika allowed a little smile. She wouldn't gloat over her competitors yet, but she couldn't help feeling pleased with herself. Each florist was assigned a specific footprint for their booths, and most had constructed flimsy, temporary walls to support their presentations. Few of those walls rose more than six feet.

The walls of Anika's booth were eight feet tall, while the waterfall majestically rose another dozen feet still. She tied off the rope and quickly secured the extra bracing to lock everything into position. Then she removed the cages around her other arrangements and stepped out of the booth to survey her work.

"Hey," the young florist to her left protested. "You can't do that."

Anika glanced at her. "Really? Did you read in the competition guidelines about height limitations?"

The girl hesitated, looking a bit less sure of herself. "I don't read, but no one builds up that high."

"So I should limit myself based on your lack of imagination?"

The girl nodded, looking relieved that Anika understood. "We all do."

The older florist from the booth on the right approached them, craning her neck up at the waterfall of flowers. They really were impressive, with the changing colors of the fountain waters splashing directly behind them.

The long chains of alternating colors made a rippling effect. At the top she'd used blue and white love-in-a-mist blossoms, their delicate, misty bracts lending a sense of watery spray. Lower down, she'd woven in white edelweiss and a lovely, rare strain of white chamomile, with ruby-red hearts that added delicious splashes of color. Near the bottom, she'd mixed in a large number of different flowers to create a breathtaking burst of blues, reds, and yellows, as if the waterfall was splashing colors in every direction.

Following that waterfall of color down to her booth, spectators could enjoy her other presentations. The walls of her platform were adorned with layers of tulips in nine vibrant colors, framed by flowering green ivy and creepers of sweet pea in delicate pinks and purples. She'd worked vibrant violets, deep blue morning glories, and white jasmine up over a series of arced trellises across the center of the booth. She'd then woven other petals into vines across the open roof, forming a subtle pattern of colors that hopefully hinted at a brilliant autumn sky, close to sundown.

All that work merely framed the centerpiece. Anika had built a replica of the huge fountain splashing so dramatically nearby. She'd built the framework using elbling grape vines. Each level of the fountain was built using different flowers. Pale rose snapdragon formed the bottom, followed by yellow roses for the second. Next came brilliant galliardia, their yellow petals surrounding maroon hearts, followed by blue cornflowers, purple crocus, and finally yellow-and-black pansies.

The result seemed to suck in her gaze. The loud splashing of the real fountain so close behind her booth reinforced the illusion, and she smiled with a deep sense of pride. She'd built something amazing. She had never imagined anything could rival the sheer thrill of unrestrained bash fighting, but staring at her breathtaking booth came awfully close.

With those delicate petals, she would crush all competition.

Flanking that marvelous centerpiece hung wreaths woven into long chains or delicate crowns, and bouquets that burst with rich color and delicate aromas. Those last items, along with some smaller arrangements in vases that she still needed to unbox were items she planned to sell to any willing buyers. Those interested in purchasing her larger arrangements would have to wait until after the judging.

"Don't ignore me," the angry florist to her left said loudly, striding a couple steps closer and pointing a finger at Anika.

That kind of confrontation was all too easy for Anika to deal with. She was a battle maiden, so there was nothing this frail little florist could do or say that could possibly threaten her.

So she moved toward the other woman, her expression calm but her eyes cold. "I'm sorry. I didn't realize you were here to gossip instead of competing."

"I'm not gossiping."

"Well you're not working either," the older florist said with a chuckle.

Anika glanced at the young woman's booth. It was nice, displayed solid skill, but nothing about it suggested the girl had any chance of actually winning. She said, "You've got some time to finish."

"But I was . . . " the girl trailed off, her gaze flickering to Anika's amazing presentation. Then without a word she spun and rushed back to her own booth.

Not totally clueless after all.

The other woman said, "Don't be too hard on the girl. You made a very dramatic entrance." Her tone turned disapproving. "No one usually pays that much attention to the dimensions."

"Probably because you haven't presented for Crown Prince Theodor before."

"True, but we've had other festivals and some competitions for selection to decorate some of the other lords' manor houses."

"So you think Prince Theodor will have the same tastes as minor lords or local festivals? You think that an international summit will not require something a little more special?"

Anika studied the woman, whose booth was better than the younger florist's, but still not outstanding. She reminded Anika of some career soldiers she knew, people who could get the job done, but who lacked drive and imagination.

The woman nodded slowly, as if considering for the first time that maybe there were different levels of tastes. She glanced back at her booth, then over at the young florist, busily rearranging one of her bouquets.

The woman sighed. "I guess I wasn't as finished as I thought."

"That's the spirit," Anika encouraged her.

The woman grunted, then returned to her own booth. Anika hoped both of them improved their displays in the short time remaining before judging began. She would prefer winning over stiff competition, but the young florist only seemed to be making her bouquet worse.

"Never work flustered," Anika said to herself. Stress stole creativity faster than officers could stop a good bash fight.

She agreed that those women needed to improve their booths. On the other hand, she wished they possessed a bit more self-confidence. Victory could never be achieved through self-doubt and second-guessing a course of action once decided upon. History was full of examples of weaker armies winning through greater determination and simple refusal to accept defeat.

The crowd began pressing closer to Anika's booth. The tall waterfall of flowers drew them in, then the trellis and the magnificent fountain captivated them. One richly dressed noblewoman leaned over a delicate glass vase that Anika had borrowed from her mother. It stood on a small table next to the fountain, and was one of Anika's best works. The woman seemed enthralled by the arrangement.

"You have good taste," Anika told her.

"Have you considered distilling this fragrance into a perfume?"

That was a good idea. Later. "Right now I'm focused on the competition."

"You should consider it," the woman urged, standing and stepping back to look up at the waterfall of flowers again.

Anika spoke loudly to the many onlookers studying her work nearby. "Don't touch anything. I'll be right back."

Speaking of perfumes and selling her flowers would play an important role in her day, but not yet. First, scout the enemy positions. Anika began making a circuit of the other florists.

It appeared the sight of her towering flower waterfall had created even more of an impression than she'd hoped. As she circled the other booths, most of the florists were busy scrambling to figure out last minute improvements to their arrangements.

Only one woman seemed confident enough not to get caught up in the frantic activity. In her twenties, the woman was tall, with big brown eyes and long, wavy brown hair that framed a smooth face. Most men would probably consider her beautiful. She seemed to be counting on that to help her because she was dressed in a pretty, light cotton dress that showed far more shapely leg and bust than was the norm. If the judges were mostly men, the tactic might prove effective.

Her confidence looked well deserved. Her booth was built around three gorgeous arrangements that could serve as centerpieces on fine palace tables. One sprouted flowers out of a six-foot-long ceramic trough. The brilliant reds, golds, pinks, and blues of the blossoms were framed by green leaves. Another was a long, intricate woven work created exclusively from edelweiss and white roses. The lack of color served to focus the eye on the intricate weaving, and the result was quite impressive.

The one in the center was her master work. Blossoms seemed to boil out of a wide, low vase before spilling out across the table and onto the floor in a riot of lavender, snowdrops, multi-colored tulips, and half a dozen others.

Anika would have liked to study that gorgeous display longer, but the woman asked, "So you're the newcomer?" She eyed Anika with a cool and calculating gaze.

"Finally, someone who pays attention to the competition."

"Who says anyone considers you competition?" The woman sneered.

The florist in the next booth over glanced up from the flower arrangement she was completely redesigning. Barely more than a girl, she wore her shoulder-length brown hair loose. Her dress was clean but worn. She kept looking around nervously, her big brown eyes wide with near-panic as she worked.

The girl paused long enough to smile at the other woman. "You tell her, Sophie. We don't need her coming in here and causing problems."

"Don't worry about her, Maud," Sophie told her gently. "Just do your best."

Interesting. Sophie acted like an older sister, or an encouraging overseer, and Maud instantly obeyed. Anika wondered how many of the other florists already considered Sophie the sure winner. Well, they'd all be disappointed.

So Anika said, "Of course I'm competition, or all you other ladies wouldn't be scrambling to improve these everyday arrangements into something worthy of a prince."

"You're clever. I'll give you that. You got most of the girls in such a panic that they'll only make things worse."

"It's good to know that at least one person who's going to lose to me today can think deeper thoughts than their potted plants. I had worried you left your brains behind in the rest of your dress," Anika said.

Sophie glared. "It doesn't really matter what any of the other florists do today. It's not really a competition. I always win, and I'll win again."

Anika was starting to like the belligerent woman. She hadn't thought she'd encounter any real resistance. Winning against florists that were all like timid little Maud would prove nothing to herself, or to Captain Ilse. Beating Sophie would make the victory far more satisfying.

"I think a lot of things are about to change," Anika said.

Sophie grunted. "We'll see. There's still plenty of time before the judges arrive, and you're the only fool who left her booth unattended."

She was right. The crowds had not seemed intent on mischief, but who knew if those self-important ladies might order a servant to abscond with an arrangement they particularly liked? They might feel entitled to it. Or one of the other florists might have an accomplice willing to vandalize other booths in order to increase her chances. That kind of deceit and treachery would make the contest far more interesting, but not if Anika ended up as the victim.

Anika didn't give Sophie the satisfaction of seeing that her comment had indeed triggered a rush of fear. She simply said, "I'll see you later."

She finished her circuit of the other booths, moving with an outward calm even though inside she was growing increasingly desperate to break into a run and returned to her booth. But she'd rather lose the competition than give

Sophie the satisfaction of seeing that her words had been effective.

Anika returned to her booth just in time. The crowd had continued to grow, and the one appreciative noblewoman had remained, clearly growing frustrated with waiting. Just as Anika arrived, her serving girl stepped right into the booth and reached for the central flower in the vase that had drawn her lady's attention.

The delicate, purple-and-gold blossom only grew far to the south. Anika doubted anyone else had one. Known as a dunkelrot, she had acquired a cutting of it the year before when on deployment near the Obrioner border.

"Don't touch that," Anika barked in her drill sergeant voice.

The maid snatched her hand away and scrambled back, retreating to cower behind her lady. The noblewoman was young enough and plain enough that she was probably desperate to find something to help her snare the attention of an eligible nobleman who might otherwise overlook her.

"What is that flower, girl?" the noblewoman demanded. In her impatience, she resorted to an imperious tone that probably helped her get whatever she wanted. It made Anika want to toss her into the fountain.

"That's the secret ingredient in a new line of irresistible perfumes I'll be bringing to market in the near future," Anika told her.

Of course, once she did produce perfume, she wasn't sure she'd be willing to market to self-important ladies, who no doubt lacked the self-respect to even wrestle with their intended husbands. The thought of helping such women surrender without any kind of fight whatsoever sickened Anika, but her battle plan required she perform the duties of a friendly florist, so she'd play the part.

The noblewoman looked affronted, but another richly

dressed woman, likely the wife of a wealthy merchant, stepped closer with an eager expression. "That sounds wonderful. I would like to purchase the recipe. My husband can get it to all the markets, all across Granadure."

The first woman exclaimed, "And he would charge a hundred times more than it's worth, while only paying this poor fool a pittance for the recipe. No. I will purchase the entire stock, and your husband can come speak to me about marketing it."

Four other rich merchant women pushed through the thick crowd and added their own offers to purchase the perfume recipe. At first, Anika figured they were simply looking for entertainment to while away the time until the prince arrived, but as the bidding continued to quickly rise, she realized they were serious.

More than that, those women knew the perfume market far better than Anika. They must have been inspecting her work not out of idle curiosity like the other gawking locals. Thorn and blossoms, those ladies had been scouting potential targets. Now that they'd identified the target, they were launching their own form of assault.

She had never imagined rich, pampered ladies might be capable of such sophisticated battlefield strategies, but once she recognized their tactics, she immediately felt a sense of calm settle over her. She understood battle, even though they were fighting with words and wealth instead of hammers and rock-hard fists.

They would not find her an easy target. She said nothing as they bid, but let them talk over each other while she watched and learned the rules of the strange new form of verbal combat.

She knew rich women loved perfume, but most of the fragrances she had ever smelled turned her stomach. Those rich merchant women had recognized that Anika's precious flower could actually produce a unique perfume. Anika hadn't spent much time exploring perfumes, but with some experimentation, and by combining other flowers with complementary scents, she decided she could probably produce a perfume worthy of the prices being offered.

And those women were offering a lot. After their initial flood of exploratory offers, they seemed to feel they'd established positions of strategic strength and settled in for a serious bidding war. As Anika studied them, she noted with approval how their stances shifted subtly.

One woman's lips kept curling into a fighting snarl, which she couldn't quite keep suppressed. Another kept her face impassive, her emotions in reserve like concealed weapons. The eyes of the third were alight with battle lust, an expression Anika understood all too well.

By krokus, she had found a group of battle maidens among that crowd of useless commoners. Anika had never imagined people could throw around so much money on nothing more than the promise of an eventual recipe. As the offers shifted from silver to gold, then to lots of gold, Anika found it hard to believe they were serious.

They were. She recognized three of the ladies caught up in the bidding. One in particular was a woman not to be ignored. The mature woman was dressed in gold-trimmed finery, her fingers dripping with enormous rings. She was Lady Oberon. She and her husband were the richest merchants outside of Edderitz, and she bid with confidence that might rival General Wolfram's legendary calm on the battlefield.

Finally, when the amounts being offered reached a level that Anika doubted they'd ever be honored, she raised her hands and said loudly, "Please, my ladies. When I complete the perfume, I'll bring samples to each of you. Then you can submit your best bid."

They didn't like the idea, but Anika would never concede the rules of engagement to them and lose all advantage. At the moment she still held the high ground and had waited for the initial bidding to rise high enough that none of the ladies could afford to offer any less when she presented an actual perfume. She alone knew the secret to that special flower. When she didn't change her mind, they grudgingly conceded and ordered their maids to write their names and addresses on parchment for Anika.

The women dispersed after that, moving on to hunt for easier prey. Anika watched them go, her mind whirling as she clutched with trembling fingers the papers with their names. Would those women really pay such enormous amounts for perfume? The thought was so foreign, she could scarce process it, and she kept breaking into astonished grins.

If she could find someone to help her develop that perfume, she might just secure more money than she ever dreamed possible. Anika had enough for her needs, so the wealth didn't tempt her as much as it probably would most girls. Her needs were modest. As long as she had granite to fuel her Petralist powers, opportunities to bash fight, and the hope of finding a man strong enough to wrestle her like she dreamed, she'd be fine.

Still, that potential fortune triggered a new dream. If she could indeed win it, she could provide for her parents for the rest of their lives, no matter where or for how long she and Erich were deployed with Captain Ilse.

Assuming she won the competition.

She hadn't come to the competition with the thought of selling perfume, but heiderkraut, not even Erich was daft enough to ignore the offer of that much gold. Anika paced across the front of her booth, so distracted by her thoughts that she barely managed to smile her thanks to onlookers who congratulated her on her impressive work.

Then without warning, a thickset man with a blocky face lunged out of the crowds, hefting a heavy mallet in one hand as he leaped toward Anika's beautiful flower fountain.

He timed his assault for the moment Anika was just turning in the other direction to offer a flower to a young girl.

Her well-honed battle instincts kicked in almost before she realized what was happening. Anika lunged across the space and caught the man's hand just as he was swinging a mighty blow that would have shattered her centerpiece. Anika tapped granite, her powers roaring through her along with an explosive anger.

The man looked shocked to meet resistance. He no doubt expected Anika to scream and run away at the first sight of danger. He definitely hadn't counted on her possessing granite-fueled strength.

The man gasped as she wrenched the mallet out of his hands and lifted him off the ground by the front of the shirt. He smelled of alcohol, and his voice slurred a bit as he shouted in her face, "Cheater! No one could build all this alone."

Anika had no idea who the man was, and at that moment she didn't care. She pulled him closer and said, "I did it all. Let me show you what else I can do."

Anika threw him.

She planned to toss him up through the splashing waters of the fountain and over the nearest shop fronts. On the back side of that building was a feed yard that was usually piled high with hay. He'd most likely survive the fall, but wouldn't dare return to bother her again.

Unfortunately, when she cocked back her arm to throw, he grabbed it. His puny grip wasn't enough to stop her, but it did throw off her aim. Howling with fear, the man smashed through Anika's flowery waterfall in a spray of brilliant blossoms. Instead of plunging through the colored waters of the fountain, he instead crashed into its central stone base.

The fountain shattered.

4

## BE CAREFUL WHAT YOU WISH FOR. YOU MIGHT JUST GET IT.

"Oh, heiderkraut," Anika muttered, disgusted that she'd let that weak, useless excuse for a man throw off her aim. What would Captain Ilse think?

While she stared at the hundreds of blossoms erupting into the air from her shattered waterfall feature, everyone else seemed more concerned about the smashed fountain. Spectators gasped in horror as the enormous fountain toppled as if in slow motion. The sharp cracking of breaking stone echoed around the square, and the powerful waters sprayed shards of broken stone in every direction, scattering everyone.

Florists, spectators, and shoppers all fled, screaming as the fountain crashed down onto many of the colorful booths. The biggest section flattened Sophie's entire shop, sending her tumbling across the plaza in a wave of multicolored water. The collapse seemed to accelerate at that point, and the din echoed like thunder back and forth across the square as water and stone shattered most of the floral competition.

It turned out there really was a Water Moccasin actively driving the waters high into the air, but the man must have been distracted because it took him four eternal seconds to react. Once he did, he quickly contained the floodwaters and drew them back into a controlled column.

The damage was already done. The plaza was covered in broken flowers. As the Water Moccasin drained the water from the sodden leaves, many of the blossoms crumbled. The scent of thousands of broken flowers filled the square with a wild, humid scent that was remarkably pleasant. Anika had never supposed that disasters could smell so good.

Silence settled over the square, but for the constant gurgle of the now-controlled waters. A loud, commanding voice broke the silence a moment later, booming with Longseer enhancement.

"What by the Tallan's blessed name is going on here?"

Crown Prince Theodor strode into the square, followed by his huge retinue of aides, soldiers, and judges. He presented an imposing figure. Tall, with broad shoulders and chiseled good looks, the prince was known as a man of action and integrity. He scanned the square with thoughtful blue eyes. He wore the silver-trimmed, blue uniform of his house guard under a fine, crimson, calf-length jacket.

Anika watched him come with growing panic. She had not meant to break the fountain. She'd only been defending her property. What would they do to her for wrecking the competition?

While she still gaped at the approaching prince, mouth open in silent denial, the man who had attacked her stumbled up out of a pile of debris and staggered away in a clumsy run.

Someone shouted, "There he goes! He's responsible."

The prince shouted, "Seize that man!"

Before the hapless fellow could take four more steps, three of the prince's Wingrunners blurred across the square and seized him. That seemed to break the silence, and the crowds rushed in from every side, angry fists raised, voices clamoring for justice.

Anika watched the proceedings with astonishment. It definitely was the man's fault, but she was the one who threw him. She had allowed that drunken fool to throw off her aim, but bringing that up would be tactical suicide.

The prince called for order, and silence fell as the Wingrunners dragged the terrified man to stand before him. The prince commanded, "Explain yourself."

The hapless fellow burst into tears and exclaimed, "I didn't mean to destroy everything. I only wanted to give Lulu a better chance of winning. She deserves a break."

Anika had no idea who Lulu was. She wondered if the girl had any idea what the idiot had planned. Had she conspired with him?

The prince glanced around the square. "Where is this Lulu?"

The angry young florist who had the booth next to Anika's crept out of the crowd, looking terrified. Although the Water Moccasin had drained the water out of everyone's clothing, her dress and hair looked bedraggled, her makeup running in streaks down her face.

"Do you know this man?" the prince asked her in a gentle voice.

"He buys flowers from me sometimes," she stammered, her voice barely above a whisper.

The idiot attacker stared at Lulu with unabashed adoration. "I thought maybe you'd notice me if I helped you win."

The girl stood tall and gave the man a withering look. She threw out her hand toward the shattered fountain. "You destroyed everything! That's not helpful!"

"I didn't mean to break the fountain. A woman intercepted me and threw me out of her shop."

"And through the fountain?" Prince Theodor laughed. "Who is this mighty florist?"

As the man turned toward Anika and several hundred pairs of eyes followed his gaze and settled on her, she strode toward the prince, head high, refusing to let anyone see how terrified she felt. She might be disqualified, but she would face her fate with courage.

"You threw this man into the fountain?" the prince asked when Anika drew near, his expression mostly neutral, but his eyes twinkled with good humor.

Anika saluted as a battle maiden, her right fist snapping up, then dropping to her heart before she made a short bow. "I didn't mean for that to happen, my lord. The fool attempted to destroy my shop. I removed him. I should have aimed better. I'm afraid I was distracted."

The prince chuckled. "A battle maiden presenting as a florist? Is that your booth, the only one still standing?"

Only then did Anika realize he was right. The collapsing fountain and bursting floodwaters had targeted the far side of the square, but all of the other booths had been caught in the disaster. The booths closest to hers had suffered the least damage, but none of them were protected by a solid framework like hers.

"It is," Anika said.

Prince Theodor gently took her arm and made a gallant half-bow. "Would you present it?"

"Of course," Anika said quickly, swallowing her surprise that the prince hadn't ordered her banished or stripped of rank.

She rushed back to her booth, followed by the prince, trailed by his aides and the judges. When he got a good look at it, the prince whistled softly. "That's a remarkable design. What is your name?"

She stood to attention and saluted again. "Anika. First fist of the battle maiden squad, your highness."

One eyebrow rose slightly, the only sign Prince Theodor allowed of his surprise. He took her hand and shook it warmly. "I must admit my surprise at discovering a first fist is also a floral genius. You do your unit great honor, Battle Maiden Anika. Congratulations. You just won the contract to supply my summer palace with all the floral arrangements and decorations for the summit."

A gasp rippled across the square, followed by half-hearted applause.

Anika barely heard it, barely retained enough presence of mind to salute again and mumble her thanks. Her voice didn't seem to be working properly, and her thoughts were spinning so fast, she could barely think.

She'd won!

She'd won?

It seemed impossible that somehow victory had snatched defeat away at the last second. She had felt supremely confident she would win, but not like this. Somehow the prince's summary decision cheapened her efforts.

The judges approached, looking unhappy, but trying not to show it. Their leader, an immaculately-dressed gentleman with graying, brown hair and weak blue eyes dared protest. "Excuse me, your honor, but shouldn't we reschedule the competition to give the other florists a chance to repair the damage?"

Prince Theodor shook his head. "I regret the disaster, but it ended up simplifying things. We don't have time. I need a florist now, and I need someone with the resilience and creative thinking to get the job done. Anika is clearly that person. Have you ever seen designs like this?"

He waved a hand at her booth. Although the waterfall feature was destroyed, the rain of flowers down over the booth had only added to the brilliant colors of the ceiling.

The judge stepped into Anika's booth, trailed by five other judges. They spent a moment inspecting her designs and quickly conferring. While Prince Theodor looked on, a little smile began tugging at the corner of his mouth. Finally he asked, "Well?"

The judge returned and, apparently trying to rescue a bit of pomp amid the abbreviated ceremony declared solemnly, "My lord, Prince Theodor, our initial inspection concurs with your esteemed opinion. This booth does indeed display talent and ingenuity commensurate with the highest levels of craft, as expected in such an important competition."

"Good," Prince Theodor said with a smile in his voice. "Thank you for such a thorough inspection." When the man started to speak again, the prince raised a hand to forestall him and said, "I appreciate all you're prepared to do for me. Please, just award her the contract."

"Very well. I cede to your will and judgment," the judge said, making a formal bow.

"Thank you." The prince shook Anika's hand one more time and said, "I look forward to seeing more of your creations."

Then he turned and raised a hand to the crowds ringing them. When he spoke, his rich, deep voice easily reached everyone in the square, but yet somehow it still sounded intimate, personal, as if he was speaking to Anika alone.

"Thank you all for joining us today. This has been an eventful morning, and I'm grateful no one was seriously injured. Please continue to share your legendary hospitality with our international guests. Your goodness and grace makes me proud to live here among you."

The crowds cheered wildly. Many waved flags, while others saluted, standing tall for their beloved prince. He moved through the crowd, shaking hands, smiling, greeting people like old friends. Then, trailed by his aides, soldiers, and officials, he disappeared up the street beyond the judgement hall.

After he departed, the lead judge huffed indignantly and said, "I have never witnessed such abandonment of protocol in all my days."

He glanced at the other judges. Most of them also looked unhappy to have missed their moment of glory, but there was obviously nothing they could do. The prince had made a decision.

One of the judges, a large woman whose many layers of clothing added to her bulk, but not in flattering ways said, "It really is a beautiful arrangement. Who knows, she might have won anyway."

"This is all highly irregular," the lead judge grumbled again. Then he sighed loudly and fixed Anika with a hard look. "Young woman, we usually interview each presenter as part of the judging to ensure you can fulfill the contract. This summit is a huge opportunity and also a mighty responsibility. We cannot accept anything short of excellent performance."

"I won't fail," Anika assured him. She was still struggling to process the crazy turn of events.

The lead judge held her gaze and warned, "You'd better not. You have five days to procure all of your materials. I'll expect to see you at the palace tomorrow to begin planning. I don't expect you'll be required to decorate all eighty-seven rooms."

Another judge, a tall, thin man with permanent crease

marks between his brows said in a nasal voice, "Certainly not. No, not more than sixty."

The large woman added, "Plus the banquet hall, the formal hall, and the patios."

The lead judge nodded. "And of course you must enhance the formal gardens. You'll have three days to complete the work once you begin."

Only her unbreakable resolve not to show weakness in front of any man kept Anika on her feet. She wanted to faint, or maybe run away screaming. Sixty rooms in three days? Plus those other areas? The words echoed again and again in her mind, so loud she completely missed the lead judge's next words.

The plump, over-wrapped woman said, "You'll receive the full amount of the funds allocated to the effort when you arrive for planning tomorrow." She gave Anika an encouraging smile. "Good luck."

Anika didn't hear anything else they said. The plaza seemed to be swaying, and she felt sick. There was no possible way she could ever get all that work done.

She'd won, but had she also doomed herself?

## 5

## WHEN ALL YOU'VE GOT TO LOSE IS EVERYTHING

The next couple of hours passed in a blur for Anika. She only dimly noted Healers tending the many people injured in the disaster, or the workmen clearing away the rubble. Many spectators soon left the rubble-strewn square, while the other florists wandered through the rubble of their booths, looking numb.

Anika wanted to work on the seemingly insurmountable problem she now faced, but couldn't spare any time. Noble-women and the wives of rich merchants thronged her shop, clamoring to purchase anything and everything. The prince had awarded her the contract to decorate his summer palace, so they were desperate to procure one of her award-winning pieces.

No doubt they planned to gloat over less-fortunate acquaintances. She could imagine them saying with casual airs, "Oh, that piece was designed by Anika, the prince's florist."

She had no idea how much the pieces might be worth, and she was too distracted to engage in intense haggling, so she used the same tactic that had worked so well earlier for the perfume. She said nothing and let the ladies outbid each other.

The fiercest bidding revolved around her centerpiece fountain, and the numbers escalated to mind-boggling levels. Finally Lady Oberon silenced all the other bidders by simply stating she would double the current highest offer. The bid was so ridiculous that the other ladies ceded the piece to her.

The woman regarded them all with imperious superiority as her servant counted out a huge number of coins to Anika, and a pair of burly workers hauled the prize away.

As fierce bidding continued, many of the other florists gathered in a silent ring, witnessing Anika's good fortune. Maud wept openly, as did several of the others. No doubt they had hoped for brisk sales, even if they didn't win, but now all of their flowers were gone and they would walk away with nothing.

Anika felt bad about that, but she wasn't sure what to do. In combat, those who lost did not win. Still, she hadn't wanted to impoverish them, only to defeat them.

But had she also defeated herself? She couldn't imagine how she could fulfill the contract alone. She longed to ask the other florists how any of them had hoped to complete such a mountain of work. Surely there were tricks, but Anika did not know them. Unfortunately, it was not the right moment to ask them a favor. Many were in shock. Some looked at her angrily, while others simply wept, and the rest stared at the money flowing into Anika's hands with open jealousy.

She simply didn't have time to figure it out. She worked in a frenzy, answering questions and responding to bids as wealthy women jostled around her, shouting for a chance to get at her flowers.

The one thing she refused to sell was the one vase containing the rare flowers that she might use to develop her perfume. Several ladies offered huge sums for that bouquet, but they were the same women who had wanted the perfume. Anika maintained enough sense of mind to keep it from them.

That only seemed to drive up the value of everything else. One noblewoman from Edderitz, in town for the summit, purchased the entire sunset trellis for nearly as much as Lady Oberon had paid for the fountain center-piece. The other eager women snatched up everything else, right down to the rows of tulips hanging from the walls.

Finally, after what felt like hours, they left Anika alone in an empty booth with her one precious vase and two new, heavy money pouches, filled to bursting, weighing down her pack. She felt exhausted, and tapped just a bit of granite. The rippling power of her Petralist strength refreshed her instantly. She had never imagined she might need such relief, had never considered sales could feel like such a full-contact job, even though the fighting was done with words and coin instead of fists and swords.

Sighing with relief, Anika stepped out of her empty booth. "Praise the Tallan's blessed memory I don't have to deal with that lot every day."

The early afternoon sun was warming the square. Anika breathed deep, enjoying the peace and relative quiet. The square still smelled like flowers and fresh-broken stone, mingling with the scents of fresh bread and meat pies wafting across the square from the inn. The scents set her stomach rumbling and she decided to find some food on the way home.

First she needed to deal with the other florists.

They had waited, silently watching the buying frenzy, and it appeared they'd used the time to decide to blame

Anika for their misfortune. They scowled at her, arms crossed, standing in loose ranks. She felt impressed. Defeat had helped them coalesce into an almost-unit. What could they accomplish if they worked together more often?

Sophie stood at the front and she stepped forward, expression furious. "Enjoying your ill-gotten gains, brute?"

The other girls muttered angrily. Before that day, Anika might have embraced the urge to tap granite and scatter the fools. Not today. Now she looked on them with new understanding. They'd suffered unexpected defeat, and that would rattle even a battle-hardened veteran, but they hadn't slunk away like cowards. No, they were standing against her.

She could respect that much about them. So she tried to explain. "I didn't plan for any of this to happen."

Sophie snorted. "You expect us to believe it was just a happy accident that you managed to destroy all of our booths just moments before the prince arrived, but your booth miraculously survived?"

"I can't help the fact that I built a stronger platform."

"Or that the entire fountain crushed mine!" Sophie shouted.

Several of the others shouted angry curses. They were whipping themselves into a frenzy. Anika wondered if they'd transform into an angry mob and try to strangle her with flowering vines.

Where had that energy hidden earlier? Seeing them pulling together, uniting in purpose was almost inspiring. Maybe a bunch of disorganized florists could become something more?

Maybe together they could decorate a prince's palace.

The thought struck her mind like lightning. Anika nearly gasped, but that would only encourage Sophie in the wrong direction. She didn't dare escalate the situation.

She'd assumed she would be able to celebrate success of phase one of her battle plan when she won the contract, but so far she felt only panic. All during the sales frenzy, her mind had whirled with the growing certainty that she'd set herself up for eventual failure. Like an over-enthusiastic unit pushing too deep into enemy territory only to find itself surrounded, its defeat guaranteed.

Now that crowd of angry florists offered the one solution to her problem. Thorns and blossoms, that solution might be the only one she could never win. The only people who could help her were the very florists she had just beaten, and who she had discounted as foolish wastes of breath.

They'd suffered temporary defeat, but she was doomed to ultimate failure.

No. She refused to accept that. Anika tried to deflect their anger. "Why don't you ask Lulu about the man who attacked my booth?"

Lulu stepped out of the crowd. She had clearly been weeping, and looked exhausted, but defiant. The girl had some spirit, at least. "I don't know that man. I've barely seen him. We've talked about it, and we think his excuse was weak."

That was annoying, but not surprising. No one wanted to admit bad things happened by chance. Better to invent an explanation that pointed blame at the person you wanted to hate.

"What?" Anika asked. "Share your ideas. Do you suppose I hired him to let me throw him into the fountain?"

"Maybe," Lulu said, and by the expressions of several of the other ladies, they'd considered exactly that.

Anika barked a laugh, cutting through that idea before it could seriously take root. "Why would I concoct such a ridiculous plan? I didn't need that fool to win the competition honestly."

"But you didn't," Sophie snarled.

"The prince made his choice. I can't change that, but I can offer you an opportunity to help make things right."

"How?" Sophie demanded suspiciously as the other ladies drew a bit closer. Their need made them interested despite themselves.

"There's plenty of work to do. I agree that today turned out crazy, so I'm offering a chance for you to come assist me."

Sophie laughed, a harsh, mocking sound. "Oh, so you've realized you're hopelessly outclassed? You think we'll let you pay us pennies to help you win honor and wealth that should be ours?"

"I'm offering you a chance to participate," Anika tried to explain, fighting down a growing urge to throw Sophie over the judgment hall. She had plenty of money from sales of her arrangements, plus the funds she'd receive from the palace. She could pay the girls well for their help.

"I can pay you--" she tried to explain.

Sophie shouted, "Forget it! We don't want your charity. Let's see how much the prince loves you after you humiliate him in front of the international summit. You'll never dare sell another flower in this city after that."

The other girls shouted agreement. Sophie was too angry and held too much influence with the other florists. Without her, Anika felt convinced she could win at least some of them over.

With Sophie present, she had no chance.

Anika wanted to try again, to argue, to convince them. She needed them and they needed her, but it was obvious their anger was too fresh, their disappointment too all-consuming.

So she said, "Think about it."

Then she turned and marched away, ignoring Sophie's taunting calls that the annoying woman threw after her.

As she strode home, her last vase of flowers clutched in her arms, she considered the situation. Yes, she'd won the first phase, but how could she have failed to realize the full scope of the next phase of strategic advancement?

She'd heard General Wolfram lecture on the challenges that faced victorious forces after the battle was won. Many times those challenges far exceeded the initial problem of battle. That was certainly proving true for Anika. She needed help. She faced zero percent chance of success without it, but the florists had rejected her.

Who else could she turn to?

Not Erich. If she went to him, he'd laugh until he fainted from lack of air.

Not her squad. The battle maidens could face any armed opponent with courage, but most of them lacked any skill at the delicate art of decoration and floral arrangements.

Only one person possessed the creativity that might help, but Anika hesitated. She marched back and forth through the streets of the city all afternoon, trying to come up with some other solution, some way to avoid the choice she knew she had to make.

Eventually she had to admit there was no other option.

She felt terrified, trapped by her predicament. She had to succeed or she'd embarrass the prince and dishonor her family. To succeed, she had to risk the future career she so desperately wanted.

There was no other way.

So she went in search of Captain Ilse.

## 6

## GREAT REWARDS OR GREAT FAILURES

Anika reached Captain Ilse's office in the military compound just prior to the dinner bell. Ilse did not command a regular troop stationed at the base, so her office was not situated in the command building. Instead, she'd been granted a lovely little cottage on the grounds of the general's quarters. The peaked-roof, two-story cottage was freshly painted in bright yellow, with the exposed woodwork stained dark brown. Someone had added rose-colored curtains in the windows. Those seemed out of place for military housing, and Anika wondered if Ilse had added them to make any potential spies second-guess if they'd found the right location.

Anika paused at the doorway, trying to settle her thoughts. She tried to focus on the fact that if she succeeded in her floral mission, she'd demonstrate leadership to the wily captain. But her thoughts kept turning to her fears that Ilse might be angry that she hadn't scheduled her test to apply for the elite team. If the captain was irked enough with her, she might refuse to offer any advice, and Anika could think of no one else to turn to.

But she hardened her resolved, schooled her expression, and knocked confidently.

"Come." Captain Ilse called immediately.

Anika pushed open the door and stepped into the office. The space consisted of little more than a small, wooden desk and chair for the captain, two wooden chairs facing her desk, and a low cabinet with doors that probably held whatever paperwork Ilse might need. Many captains employed aids to manage visitors and handle mundane paperwork, but Anika spotted no signs that anyone but Ilse worked in the office.

Captain Ilse rose to meet her. She was only average height, a slender woman in her twenties with raven-black hair and piercing blue eyes. She moved with the grace of a warrior and with the confidence of a woman who knew exactly what she was capable of. Anika had seen her from a distance several times, but felt awed to stand face to face with the legendary captain.

Anika saluted smartly, and Ilse returned the gesture. The small office was neat, although it was obviously the entry room of the cottage, hastily refitted to act as an office. The wall behind Ilse's desk was not painted, and the room lacked finished touches, like molding round the door.

An open doorway through the rear wall led into the rest of the cottage, while a rack beside the entry door held Ilse's armor and weapons. A thin, carpeted runner covered the wooden floor down the center of the room. The space seemed far too plain for the great Captain Ilse, but she didn't seem bothered by it.

Ilse shook Anika's hand warmly and said in a friendly tone, "Finally we get to meet. Erich has told me a lot about you, Anika. I had expected to receive your application by now." She gestured Anika toward one of the wooden chairs facing her desk.

"I'm planning to apply," Anika assured her as she settled into the chair.

Ilse returned to her seat behind the desk and gave Anika an appraising look. "But you decided to invade the floral community first."

Hearing that Ilse was aware of Anika's floral assault made her suddenly nervous. Anika wasn't surprised Ilse knew, but had hoped Ilse wouldn't find out until she had already proven herself. Spoken like that, her decision sounded foolish.

Anika rushed to explain, but Ilse waved her to silence. "Relax. Erich has explained your bet, and I understand your motivation." She paused, and Anika suddenly felt self-conscious as Ilse studied her with a calculating gaze. The captain continued softly. "I applaud your decision to prove yourself, although I admit I was surprised by the manner you chose to do so."

Anika felt a wave of terror to think she might disappoint this great woman and destroy her chances of joining the elite team. "It seemed appropriate at the time."

"I'm glad you made a choice and pursued it with conviction," Ilse said. "Since you're here today, I will share with you the fact that I've been concerned you weren't yet ready to join my team."

"I'm not?" Anika asked, her voice squeaking in a way that annoyed her enormously. She found it hard to breathe, didn't think she could take rejection by Captain Ilse on top of the insurmountable challenge she faced in fulfilling her contract to the prince.

"That's not what I said," Ilse chided gently. "I said I feared you might not be. From all accounts, you're a talented bash fighter, but I need more than mindless fighters. I need quick-thinking warriors who can handle difficult situations. Flexible minds who can deal with unexpected challenges."

"I can do that even better than Erich," Anika promised.

"Perhaps, but you've never done anything but follow in his footsteps until now."

Anika wasn't sure what to say. Ilse's words confirmed Erich's worries and Anika's own darkest fears. Was Ilse going to dismiss her before she even applied for the team?

Ilse leaned forward slightly and added, "That's why I'm so pleased to hear about your success today. You stepped outside of your comfort zone, and from the accounts I received of your performance, you produced exceptional work."

"Thank you," Anika stammered, barely believing the words.

"Although we'll need to address your abysmal performance in throwing that poor fool into the fountain."

Anika cringed. Ilse was exceptionally well informed, although that shouldn't surprise anyone. "I failed to account for his grabbing my arm," she admitted.

"Such an oversight can be corrected in the future with proper training," Ilse said, leaning back in her chair. "I prefer to focus on your victory, especially since your win today offers potential benefits to my own responsibilities."

"Really?" Anika asked, emboldened by Ilse's last statement. She'd train harder than ever if the captain only gave her the chance.

Ilse nodded. "Indeed. May I assume you are here because of that victory?"

"I am. Phase one was successful, despite the challenges you mentioned." Anika paused, glancing down at her hands before quickly going on. "The other florists posed little threat, but now they hate me, but I need them. I can't fulfill the contract alone."

Ilse nodded in understanding. "Remarkable how some-times even great strength will fall to simple numerical advantage and proven expertise."

Anika nodded, feeling relieved that Ilse understood, even though she felt ashamed to admit she needed a pack of disorganized, non-Petralist girls more than she did a company of granite-hardened battle maidens. Even thinking about sending in the battle maidens to help with flowers made her shudder. They'd be as successful as a stampede of cattle.

So she met Ilse's gaze and admitted, "That's why I came to see you."

"Well, there's no doubt you must fulfill your contract. No battle maiden of your caliber would ever accept defeat. Plus, I need you positioned at the palace during the summit. The prince's own guard will provide primary security, but my team has been assigned supplemental coverage to deal with exceptional threats and the potential for hostile spies or assassins."

Anika hadn't heard anything about that. It made sense, and she felt a flash of jealousy to think Erich would get to chase assassins while she struggled to figure out how to decorate everything. "I don't plan to give up."

"Good. Your presence there among the servants is perfect. You'll be in position to keep an eye out for anyone who doesn't look like they belong. One of Lukas's agents reported sighting a new Obrioner operative in Edderitz. That suggests one might try to slip into the summer palace during the summit. It'll be a tempting target, so we must assume the attempt will be made."

Anika nodded. If Obrion was holding an international summit, she didn't doubt General Wolfram would send spies to infiltrate the event.

"We'll have all of the delegates and their staff under

constant supervision, but the greatest danger is a spy trying to slip in disguised as one of the many workers or suppliers being brought in to support the summit. The palace is awash with strangers. I'm glad you'll be holding the floral flank."

"If I'm even there," Anika warned, although she felt a warm glow of hope beginning to wash away her fears of defeat. Ilse was speaking as if she considered Anika part of the team.

"You must think a little deeper," Ilse chided. "Your decision to assemble a team is exactly right. You must act as captain to a force of floral decorators. That kind of creative thinking is exactly what I look for from my team members, and you must succeed to be of use to me."

There it was, as plain as purple heiderkraut. If Anika failed, she failed double. Defeat would not only embarrass the prince and negatively impact the summit, but it would destroy Anika's chances of ever joining Ilse's elite team.

"I understand," Anika managed, pleased that she kept her voice steady.

Ilse held her gaze for a moment, before nodding. Her expression was mostly neutral, but Anika decided she picked up a hint of approval.

Captain Ilse added, "But you must take your plan to the next logical step."

"What step? The florists don't want to cooperate and they're the only ones who could do the work."

"You've led your squad of battle maidens for the past six months. Who should you always appoint as your assistant?"

"The next strongest fighter."

"And who among the florists might be the best candidate for that position?"

Anika opened her mouth to say, "None of them." But

she paused as she thought back to her brief interactions with the other girls. The truth surprised her and she exclaimed, "Sophie."

When Ilse raised an eyebrow in question, Anika explained about how Sophie was the undisputed leader of the other girls. Unfortunately, she was the one leading the others in their opposition.

Ilse leaned forward over her desk. "Your challenge is to determine what Sophie wants and how to offer that to her in such a way that she can only get it by helping you."

She let Anika think about that for a moment before adding, "I've never had anyone initiate an application like this before. I like your creativity, and I'll be watching. Keep me posted."

"I will. Thank you, Captain."

She rose, thrilled and terrified at the same time. Could she really win her place on the elite company by orchestrating a successful floral campaign in the palace?

She had no choice. Ilse had made that clear. She would accept Anika's attempt to prove she was more than a simple bash fighter, but she would not accept defeat.

The opportunity represented everything she wanted, but this mission could not be won through brute strength. She needed to figure out how to rally the florists, even though that would be the last thing they'd want to do.

Sophie was the key. The others would follow her lead, but how to accomplish that? Anika left the base, deep in thought. She paced the empty practice field, ignoring the call to dinner, despite how hungry she felt.

She let Sophie fill her thoughts. She considered everything she knew about the woman, about florists in general. Her annoyance at their lack of organization and leadership returned in a rush.

Sophie had shown leadership. That morning in the square, the florists had acted as a unit for the first time. Sophie could get them to do so again.

Suddenly Anika knew how to bring the other ladies on board.

## 7

## AN OFFER IN A GUILDED BOUQUET

Anika sat at a window booth of a small restaurant the following morning. The breakfast crowd had already eaten and left for work, but the noonday patrons would not begin to arrive for another hour or two. That left the low-ceilinged room full of tables and chairs, with booths around the outer edges, empty of other diners.

The cook and single serving girl were taking a break in the back. They had looked more relieved than annoyed when Anika ordered only a tall, frosted glass of Most. The refreshing blend of apfelsine and preiselbeere juices was her favorite morning beverage.

This morning, she barely noticed the perfectly balanced mixture of sweet and bitter flavors as she watched Sophie selling flowers on a nearby street corner.

Today the flower girl dressed a bit more modestly, with her hair held back by a simple wooden comb. She had expertly positioned her brightly painted flower cart in front of a drab, gray stone building. The splash of color drew the gaze, and her artful arrangements of flowers easily held it.

She was an experienced street seller. She smiled and

called out greetings to passersby, her presence charming and engaging. The well-practiced effort seemed to be garnering her regular sales.

And the attention of many men. Some of them clearly expected to see her and they often slowed to flirt with her. Some of them purchased flowers, while others only seemed interested in enticing her into joining them for dinner or a late-night stroll. She did an admirable job of deflecting most of those advances without offending, and most of the admirers left with a smile and a wave, clearly planning to stop for another chat tomorrow.

One fellow didn't want to take no for an answer.

He'd waited to approach her until the morning crowd had thinned. Anika had watched in growing interest as the beefy fellow became increasingly insistent. Even from a distance, it looked like he'd been drinking. His clothes might have looked fine if they weren't so wrinkled and clearly in need of a washing. It wasn't even noon yet, so Anika had to wonder if he'd just stayed up all night partying.

She didn't really care. Sophie's ready smile had faded to a look of irritation that had shifted to concern. The man grabbed at her arm, but she slipped away, her expression now bordering on panic.

Anika finished her drink, left some coins on the table, and strode out of the shop. Sophie could easily escape the man's clumsy advances, but that would mean abandoning her cart, her livelihood, and she was clearly loathe to do that.

The street was nearly empty, with no sign of the city watch. They rarely patrolled this part of town at this time of day. There was usually no need.

Sophie didn't notice Anika approaching. She was

focused on the drunk, her friendliness gone. "Get away from me. I don't want anything to do with you."

The man's leer turned annoyed and he snapped, "Oh, come on sweetie. You look lonely. Come have a drink."

Anika arrived just as he stepped around to the street side of the cart and nearly bumped into her. He looked at her with surprise that turned into delight.

"Tallan be praised! Another beauty, and a friendly one at that."

Anika slapped his reaching hand aside hard enough to stagger him a pace farther out into the street. She gave him a cold glare and declared, "Sir, you have become a nuisance. The florists are now protected by my guild and it's time for you to move on."

Sophie looked like she couldn't decide if she felt more relieved by the assistance or shocked by the bold declaration.

The man barked a laugh. "Florists don't have a guild. They're just girls looking for someone to show them a little attention."

"That's no longer the case," Anika said, not hiding her disgust.

He looked her up and down appreciatively. She wasn't wearing her battle leathers, but was dressed in her best skirt and blouse for the looming visit to the palace. "What about you then, missy? Do you need a friend?"

"I need you to leave. Now."

"Oh, don't be hasty," he said, stepping close and trying to wrap an arm around her waist.

That was so much better than if he had actually heeded her warning.

Anika tapped granite and lifted the fool off the ground by the shirt and said in a cold, deadly voice, "I never give more than one warning. Since you're too drunk to under-stand, how about I help sober you up?"

She carried the uselessly squawking fellow across the street and plunged him headfirst into a large, full rain barrel. By the quantity of bubbles, he wasn't smart enough to stop shouting stupid protests.

Anika raised him just long enough for him to suck in a coughing breath, then shoved him back down again. She repeated the process eight more times before tossing him to the curb. Soaked, bedraggled, and far more sober than before, he gasped, coughed, and cried, "Tallan's bones, woman, are you insane?"

Anika leaned over him, and as he quailed back against the curb, one hand raised for mercy, she said, "If you ever bother any of my girls again, I will remove your tongue so they don't have to listen to your idiocy ever again."

"By the Tallan's memory, I swear I won't," he promised, the words tumbling out so fast she barely understood him.

"Then get out of my sight."

She returned to Sophie while the man scrambled away, his footsteps squishing with every step. She didn't want to intimidate Sophie, so released granite.

Sophie waited for her with hands on hips, chin up, expression defiant. "There is no floral guild, and you know it."

Anika grinned. "There is now."

"Says who?"

"Me."

"Oh, and how many florists have joined your imaginary guild?"

"You'll be the first."

Sophie snorted. "You're more desperate than I thought."

"You need me as much as I need you."

"I don't need anyone," Sophie insisted. She patted her

apron. "I was just about to hit that fool with my secret weapon. It's never failed."

"What weapon?" Anika asked. She couldn't believe Sophie actually knew how to fight, but she'd welcome that surprise.

"Take a look." Sophie dipped her hand into a concealed pocket at the seam of her apron.

Anika leaned closer, intrigued. She didn't see the telltale bulge of a dagger or bludgeon behind the cloth. What weapon would a florist possess that would give her such confidence against a bully like that drunk fool?

Sophie extracted her hand and flung it toward Anika, releasing a powdery mist, almost like a handful of pollen.

Anika recoiled from the movement, but started to grin when she realized what Sophie had done. That was no weapon it was just a silly . . .

She sneezed violently. Her entire midsection convulsed, whipping her head down almost far enough to collide with her knees. She staggered and sneezed again, so hard it felt like her abdomen was tearing. Her throat felt raw, her nose sprayed snot across her feet, and she dropped to one knee, gasping, only to sneeze a third time.

She couldn't breathe, couldn't think, and only managed to keep from falling prone to the cobblestones by tapping granite. The rush of strength from her Petralist power helped clear her head.

Anika sneezed two more times in rapid succession, but they had lost their intensity. The sneezing fit passed as quickly as it had struck, and Anika managed to stagger back to her feet. If not for the strength of granite, she would have wobbled.

Sophie looked surprised by her rapid recovery. "Not bad. Even that tiny bit of exposure to sneezing powder usually renders people useless for several minutes."

Anika shook her head to clear the last vestiges of disorientation. Part of her wanted to slap Sophie, rip that apron off of her, and force her to sniff all the rest of her powder. See how she liked sneezing her stomach onto her shoes.

Sophie retreated a step from her anger, hand dipping back into the pocket, but Anika reined in her fury and held up a placating hand.

"Relax. You caught me by surprise."

Sophie chuckled. "That's the whole point. Doesn't work so well otherwise."

"I've never experienced anything like that," Anika admitted.

"One of the little secrets I've picked up over the years working the street. Several of the other girls use it too."

But not all of them. One more reason why they needed organization. Sophie was resourceful, but was still thinking like an independent girl, alone on the street without any support. Anika needed to change that.

She glanced back toward the drunk man, who had run far enough that he felt safe enough to begin shouting about the abuse he'd suffered. Maybe she should have dunked him a few more times.

Pointing at the fleeing fool, she asked, "What happens if he just collapses for a while, then gets up and attacks you once the sneezing fit stops?"

"It's possible, but rare. I threaten to hit them again, and most of the time they take off. Idiots like that are part of the price of doing business."

"They don't have to be. A guild could offer protection and assistance, help with better prices and more stable supply."

"We've managed just fine in the past," Sophie insisted, but at least she was listening.

"You're telling me you don't want to improve your situation?"

"I would have improved my situation by winning that contract from the prince. It's your fault I'm stuck out here on the street."

"Just because I received the contract doesn't mean we all can't benefit."

Sophie actually paused to consider her words before saying, "Guilds are expensive."

"I know how to raise the money to start one right."

"How? Are you going to surrender the prince's award?"

"I don't know yet how much of those funds I'll need to purchase supplies and pay the other girls who agree to help, but I have another funding source for our guild."

Anika told her about the ridiculous offers she'd received for the perfume. "If they were willing to offer that much on nothing but the promise of that scent, I'm sure once we have a finished product, final bids will end up much higher. If we negotiate the deal through our new guild, then the guild will receive commission on every sale. That'll give us ongoing income to keep the guild solvent."

Sophie looked thunderstruck by the idea. "Are you cracked? You could set yourself up for life."

Anika shrugged. "I'll still take my share. I'll be fine, and once we get our guild in place, so will you and the other girls."

Sophie paced several times around the cart, clearly struggling to believe Anika was speaking in earnest. She didn't blame her. The proposition must sound ludicrous, but it made perfect sense to Anika. She couldn't afford the weeks or months it would take to perfect a new perfume and negotiate a favorable contract for its sale and distribution.

Finally Sophie stopped in front of her and demanded, "Why?"

"Simple. I need a team. I need girls who actually know how to do the work. That means we need an organization to manage everyone. I need that same organization to manage this perfume for me and send me my cut. Why not build something that we can use to do all that and benefit everyone involved?"

"And you end up owning all of us," Sophie said.

Anika shook her head. "The guild isn't for me, Sophie. After the conference, I plan to follow a different path."

"Why build a guild then, if you're going to throw it away?"

"You weren't listening. The guild isn't for me. The guild is for you and the other girls. I will show you how to build an organization, but you have to lead it after I leave."

"Me?" Sophie gaped, looking more surprised than ever.

"Of course. The other girls already follow your lead. You're the only one who could make it work."

"You really are insane," Sophie laughed softly, her belligerence gone, replaced by bewildered joy.

"We can help each other succeed. Don't you think you can accomplish more as a guild matron than you can stuck on this street corner?"

Sophie considered her for a long moment before breaking into a warm smile. "I still don't quite believe it, but I can't see how you're planning to double-cross me. So I'm in, as long as I don't find that you've lied about anything."

"I haven't lied, and we're due at the palace in three hours."

Sophie's eyes widened, and a look of wonder spread across her face. Then she took a deep breath and said, "Then let's get to work. This stock of flowers won't last another day, so we've got two hours to sell everything."

## 8

# FEEL THE LOVE. SMELL THE ROSES.

Prince Theodor's summer palace was a grand estate known as Reizend, located in the rolling hills east of Golm. As Anika led Sophie up a wide, gently curving lane toward the palace, she fought the urge to gape. Stately trees flanked the lane, with well-manicured lawns, dotted with splashing fountains stretching out to either side.

Finally growing annoyed with herself, she stood taller and decided to treat the awe-inspiring sights like she would a visit with Captain Ilse or even the great General Wolfram. She would show respect, but not weakness. If she didn't believe she belonged there, no one else would.

"Praise Tallan," Sophie muttered when they reached the point where the lane emptied into the wide forecourt and paused to soak in the magnificent view of the palace.

It took Anika's breath away.

Reizend was a beehive of activity, with craftsmen, caterers, and workers of every kind, representing every guild, scurrying about. The enormous entry court was packed with delivery wagons and carts, with burly porters moving supplies into the towering palace. Soldiers prowled everywhere, and the entire palace thrummed with expectant energy.

The front of the palace reared above the forecourt in three majestic stories. The square, central nave was flanked by long wings that extended over a hundred yards in either direction before sweeping forward to partially encircle the court. The effect was welcoming, like a huge, architectural hug.

Anika could just make out additional, shorter buildings, extending beyond the ends of both of those majestic wings. They curved back the other way to reduce their visibility. By the vast amounts of foodstuffs being hustled toward both of them, and by the many columns of smoke rising into the still, afternoon sky from unseen chimneys, she bet those were kitchens.

She nudged Sophia and said, "Two kitchens. Think the prince really eats that much?"

Sophie shrugged. "Dishes probably get cold before they can make it from one end to the other. Makes more sense to start from either side. But why would you focus on the kitchens when there are so many more amazing sights?"

"Always watch for the most likely locations for flanking maneuvers."

Sophie shook her head and chuckled. "You're the weirdest florist I've ever heard of."

Seeing Sophie smile and only call her weird was welcome progress. Anika said, "Don't limit yourself. If you look at only what someone wants you to see, you might miss the most important elements."

"I will," Sophie promised. "But right now, I'm going to gawk at that palace.

Anika joined her. It was definitely gawk-worthy. The salmon-colored walls facing the forecourt were broken by enormous, arced windows that marched down the entire length of the palace. Through those huge windows, she caught sight of many-crystaled chandeliers and very ornate rooms. She spotted no candle brackets in the chandeliers, though. No doubt the prince employed several Solas to light them and keep the entire palace blazing bright.

The high walls facing them on three sides echoed the sounds from the bustling activity back onto Anika and Sophie, magnifying the banging of crates, stomping of horse hooves, and shouted directions. The effect only heightened the sense of urgency that drove everyone on. The scents of lumber and horses and mules mixed with smells from the cook fires and the sharper odors of paint and cleaning solutions.

Anika took a deep breath and let the sights, sounds, and smells wash over her. A little smile played across her lips as she closed her eyes and imagined herself standing in the chaotic training fields of the military base during a mock battle drill.

That helped calm her nerves, and she beckoned the still-gaping Sophie forward. "Come on. Let's find someone who can show us around and get us paid so we can start planning."

"Even with all the other girls helping, how by the Tallan's grace can we finish in time?" Sophie wondered as Anika led her toward the huge double doors of the main entryway.

They wove between tight-packed carts and wagons, avoiding workers shouldering heavy loads that threatened to block their path.

"The bigger the challenge, the greater the victory," Anika assured her. Without Sophie committed to helping, she would not have dared enter the palace. Together, they strode forward confidently. They would succeed and produce the best work the prince had ever seen. She would impress Captain Ilse and win her place in the company.

Once they entered the palace, she pulled Sophie to a halt to scan the terrain again. This would be the first position of strength where they would set the critical first impression, which they would then build upon in each additional room. The entering dignitaries would feel impressed, then amazed, and the decorations would need to reinforce those impressions at every stage.

The grand entry hall rose through all three stories of the palace, capped by a gilded dome. The white marble walls were broken by many windows, flanked by fluted columns. An enormous chandelier hung from the center of the dome, its thousands of cut crystals glowing with light that slowly shifted through subtle hues, from pure white, to yellow, to soft blue that illuminated the entire hall without becoming glaring.

They turned into the east wing, but it took a few minutes to find a steward in the blue and silver of Prince Theodor's private colors and get the man's attention. The harried young official looked the two of them over and asked, "Who are you?"

"The florist guild. Here to tour the palace and begin planning decorations."

"You have a guild now?"

"Yes, we do," Anika said, steeling herself for his objections.

Instead, the fellow blew out a relieved breath and said, "Praise Tallan. It's about time the florists organized. I don't have time to hold the hands of a bunch of terrified girls. The last florists we hired got so overwhelmed by Reizend that I could have done the work faster myself."

That assessment might be true, but it suggested they had a lot of low expectations to deal with. "That won't happen this year," she assured the man. "We need payment, a tour, and time with whoever we'll need to work with to coordinate efforts."

He seemed to appreciate the specific list. The man beckoned a nearby serving girl to them. "Take them to Lady Katrin. Good luck, florists."

Then he rushed off, acknowledging their thanks with a wave. The serving girl, who looked barely twelve years old, led them east, along the huge corridor that felt cramped with all the foot traffic. The girl moved fast, slipping with practiced ease through the crowds. She didn't seem concerned about the fact that she might lose them.

Anika wasn't about to lose their guide and have to ask directions from someone else. She wasn't sure if the girl was testing them, or if she was just a terrible guide. So Anika asked, "How good is your balance?"

Sophie tore her gaze from the beautiful frescos on the ceiling, looking confused. "What?"

"Your balance. How is it?"

Luckily Sophie didn't bother asking more questions. "It's good. I used to dance."

"Perfect." Anika tapped granite. Her body shifted to perfect lines and her skin shifted to a soft, rose hue.

"What are you doing?" Sophia asked nervously. "You can't start bashing people."

Anika grinned. "Nothing so barbaric. We're florists, remember?"

Then she took Sophie by the waist and tossed her into the air. Sophie yelped with surprise as Anika lifted her high overhead, supporting her right foot with an open hand. Sophie recovered quickly, and after an initial wobble, she straightened, settling into a poised, graceful dancer's pose, with her left leg bent, left foot braced against her right leg.

"Can you see that girl?" Anika asked.

"Yes," Sophie said with a laugh. "And everyone can see me."

She was right. The unexpected sight of a pretty florist suddenly standing high in the air drew the attention of all the people packing the hall around them. Some pointed, others laughed, a few whistled.

Sophie seemed to enjoy the attention. She spread her arms in a slow, liquid movement, as if preparing to launch into a twirling dance across people's skulls. Anika grinned and started walking. The crowds parted around them, and she spotted the serving girl about a dozen feet ahead.

The girl glanced back and her satisfied smile broke into a gape when she spotted them. It appeared she had indeed been trying to lose them. Anika couldn't imagine why, but the girl seemed to realize the game was up and she'd lost.

"Don't look up my dress, or my assistant will crush your head," Sophie warned one burly worker who stepped a bit closer to peer up at her. The man laughed until Anika raised a clenched fist, her expression cold.

Then it was his companions' turn to laugh as he wisely retreated. After that, everyone gave them plenty of space.

When they reached the waiting serving girl, Sophie said, "Don't try to disappear again, or my assistant might feel obliged to carry you by the hair."

That seemed to cow the girl. Although Anika didn't appreciate being called an assistant, she liked Sophie's tact. She would have just threatened the girl with violence, but there in the palace they needed to practice a higher level of charm.

"I'm sorry," the girl stammered quickly. "It won't happen again."

"You were told to give us the slip, weren't you?" Anika asked.

"Um . . . I don't . . . I mean . . . no," the girl protested, eyes wide with fear.

"You're a terrible liar," Sophie said, leaning forward, left leg extending gracefully, arms going wide again. Anika took the queue and lowered her to the floor.

"Please don't hurt me," the girl told Anika as she stepped closer.

"I find people who lose their tongues don't tell as many lies," Anika said softly, keeping her expression neutral.

The girl gulped, but Sophie chuckled and said, "I bet they can't tell many truths after you rip out their tongues either, do they?"

Anika shrugged. "Simplifies things, doesn't it?"

The girl looked close to panic and she said quickly, "I meant no harm. Biberach ordered me to make you late."

"And who is Biberach?" Anika asked.

"One of Lady Katrin's assistants. He helps with interior decorating."

Anika exchanged a glance with Sophie who told the girl, "We'll deal with Biberach. You just take us to Lady Katrin."

The girl curtsied then set off again, this time staying close and casting many worried glances back at Anika. While she walked, Anika wondered why anyone would want to make them late. Biberach had to be looking for some kind of tactical advantage, but she lacked enough intelligence to understand his attack pattern. Now that they were aware of the danger, they'd be ready to counter-attack.

Within a few moments, they reached a rather plain, wooden door set in the left-hand wall, near the east kitchen. The girl knocked, then ushered them into the rather cramped office on the other side.

A matronly-looking woman sat behind a desk piled with papers and scrolls. Anika assumed she must be Lady

Katrin. When she glanced up from the parchment she was reading, she met Anika's gaze with steady brown eyes. Her hair was dyed bright gold, and when she smiled, laugh lines around her mouth and eyes sprang into view.

"Ah, the florists." She rose and came around the desk to meet them.

Anika remembered that she'd seen the woman among the judges at the competition. If Lady Katrin thought anything about the proceedings unusual, she seemed to have let those worries go. She greeted Anika enthusiastically.

"I loved your work. I have high hopes for a spectacular centerpiece for the banquet table."

"We'll do our best."

She greeted Sophie just as enthusiastically. "Sophie, isn't it?"

"Yes, ma'am," Sophie said, looking surprised and pleased.

"I've been watching your work for some time. I'm thrilled to see you two together. You represent the most exciting talents in the Golm floral circles."

"Thank you," Sophie said with a little curtsy.

Anika decided she liked Lady Katrin. The woman seemed competent, enthusiastic, and well aware of people involved in crafts that interested her. "You'll get more than just the two of us this year. We represent the new florist guild, and I expect to employ all of the girls in the decorating project."

Lady Katrin clapped her hands together enthusiastically. "Perfect. I always thought the girls needed a little organization. This project will be many times larger than anything any of you have attempted before. I was worried about anyone's ability to pull it off alone." She held Anika's gaze and her expression turned serious. "I must impress upon you the gravity of the opportunity we all face. This summit is of enormous importance to the prince. Reizend is the perfect location, and I will not allow anything but your very best work. Anything less would insult this wondrous place and dishonor the prince."

Sophie looked a bit nervous, but Anika appreciated the woman's honesty. She clearly loved Reizend. Leaders who led with passion and commitment always inspired greater commitment from those who followed. This project was becoming a substantial mission on every front, even better than she had hoped.

So she said, "I agree completely."

"Good. Your timing is perfect. I just received word that my assistant, Biberach, is ready to begin planning decorations. I nearly had to let him start without you."

Anika met Sophie's gaze again, and things started to make more sense. Sophie told Lady Katrin, "Well, I'm glad we're on time so he doesn't have to worry about our part of the work."

"Me too." Lady Katrin said. "I cannot afford any confusion about responsibilities."

Anika got an idea and said, "You clearly love this palace, my lady. Why don't you join us for the tour? That way you can ensure we all understand our duties."

"I was going to leave that to Biberach, but you're right. I'd love to walk with you." She pointed at a square, iron-bounded, wooden chest, each side almost as long as Anika's forearm. "Your payment is there. I believe you'll find it more than sufficient. I expect only the best, and I've ensured you'll have the funds you need to provide it. You can pick it up on your way out."

Sophie's eyes widened in wonder as she stared at the chest. She coughed, tried to suppress it, which only made the coughing worse. Anika pounded her on the back hard enough to make her stagger. She appreciated the chance to work through her own astonishment. She'd seen a chest of money almost that big once. It had held the entire company's monthly pay.

"Thank you," she managed to say to Lady Katrin, proud that she kept her voice calm. "I'm sure it will be adequate. We have exciting plans."

"Excellent. Let's get to it then, shall we?" Lady Katrin swept out of the office, with Anika and Sophie in tow.

They first headed to the formal, great hall where the delegates would meet in conference on the first floor of the central section of the palace. Lady Katrin easily pushed open the huge, double doors. The tall, arched doors were constructed of thick iron, painted king's blue, divided into twelve raised panels on each side. Each panel was inscribed with seals and sigils, and the entire doorway was surrounded by intricate scrollwork. The doors must have each weighed half a ton, but they were perfectly balanced on thick hinges and swung inward at barely a touch from lady Katrin.

The hall was tiled in alternating black and white ceramic squares. The exterior wall was broken by a dozen arched windows that overlooked the formal gardens behind the palace, while the opposite interior wall held tall mirrors that reflected the view and made the huge room feel even more spacious and open. The white-painted walls and ceiling were broken by golden scrollwork and brass murals depicting scenes from Grandurian history.

A long, polished, mahogany table ran down the center of the room, surrounded by red-padded armchairs. A rather scrawny looking fellow, wearing an over-starched uniform stood at the far end of the table. His brown hair was styled more carefully than many women Anika knew, and he was stroking a wispy beard, as if trying to encourage it to grow into something grand.

He spotted them immediately, and he couldn't quite hide an expression of disbelief at seeing Anika, Sophie, and Lady Katrin arriving together. He changed it to one of fawning eagerness as Lady Katrin approached.

"My lady, I'm surprised to see you here. I thought you were busy with other duties."

"Don't worry about me, Biberach," she replied, seemingly oblivious to his initial displeasure. "These are the florists, here to decorate the palace for the conference. You don't have to begin the work alone after all."

"Wonderful," he said as he made a stiff bow to Anika, but by his tone, he clearly didn't feel wonderful.

Anika immediately disliked the fool. Too bad the beautiful windows were all closed. Throwing him out would have to wait. She reminded herself to learn the proper etiquette for throwing someone out a window at the Reizend. Did she need to raise a pinky finger, or curtsy until they hit the ground, or something?

For the moment, she only said, "We're ready to get to work."

"You don't need to take so much time out of your busy day, my lady," he protested.

"Not to worry. I can make time. Sometimes you take on more than you have to. I'm glad we're all together to ensure there's no confusion. There's far too much to do for that."

"I agree," Sophie said smoothly. If she disliked Biberach, she concealed her feelings well. She gave him a warm smile and gestured around the room. "Shall we begin?"

Sophie proved her worth immediately. She knew all the right questions to ask, and Lady Katrin's approving smile grew wider the longer they talked. Biberach tried to offer alternate suggestions, but they lacked Sophie's grand vision, and he was overruled every time.

As his frown deepened, Anika felt like maybe she understood the man. He clearly wanted the job of decorating the palace, which would explain his petty attempt to delay them. As long as he understood his place from that point on, she'd have no problem with him.

They discussed the best types of flowers to accentuate the beautiful, formal setting, and where best to place them. Sophie suggested a variation of her masterful centerpiece that had been destroyed by the fountain. Anika supported the idea, and Lady Katrin agreed.

They moved next to the grand ballroom with its high, vaulted ceiling where evening events would take place. Sophie suggested several large, flowering shrubs placed strategically around the walls to help facilitate semi-private discussions. The idea won immediate approve.

Lady Katrin said, "And Anika, what do you think of recreating that beautiful waterfall effect down the east wall over there?"

"It's the perfect place for it," she admitted, calculating the vast number of flowers and the hours that one arrangement would consume.

"The waterfall was destroyed rather easily in the square," Biberach pointed out. "Perhaps some woven vines instead?"

"Nonsense," Lady Katrin said. "That would never do."

"I hadn't designed the waterfall to withstand getting a man thrown through the center of it," Anika admitted.

Sophie added, "And we don't plan to have that happen during the summit." Her eyes seemed to ask, "Do we?"

"Tallan's blessed memory, let's avoid that at all costs," Lady Katrin said with a laugh.

Next came the music room, complete with a grand piano

in one corner, a smaller spinet piano on the opposite side near racks of exquisite instruments of more variety than Anika had ever seen, and several she had never heard of. A huge pipe organ consumed much of the western wall, the dozens of glittering brass pipes filling the room with warm, golden reflections. The glossy floor was made of different-colored woods, set in a geometric pattern like interlocking, three-dimensional boxes. The subtle green of the walls highlighted the gilded paint of the trim and the intricate scrollwork that crept across the ceiling.

The next two hours passed in a blur of overloaded senses. As they explored most of the opulent palace, every room was different, each requiring a different approach to properly decorate. They were all so beautiful that Anika found herself wondering why they bothered adding floral arrangements to some of them. In others, the soft, living colors of the flowers would contrast with the cold beauty of gold, brass, and crystal, making the space feel more inviting and perhaps just a bit less formal and intimidating.

She and Sophie alternated taking the lead in the discussions. Sophie had an eye for detail, and more direct experience to draw upon. Anika could scan a room and spot tactical advantages of unique placements more quickly, and her creative flair pleased Lady Katrin in equal measure to how much it annoyed Biberach.

The fellow grew downright surly when Lady Katrin suggested he take over transcribing notes while she brainstormed with Anika and Sophie. Anika loved reminding him to include points that he seemed willing to forget, and she regularly double-checked his work. When he realized she could read, he stopped trying to mis-record the plan. His attitude would definitely need to be addressed, but she decided to wait for a quiet moment when Lady Katrin was not around.

After completing the tour of the downstairs, they reviewed the grand staircase up to the second floor. The tour continued through part of that floor, but took far less time. The spaces would be frequented by fewer quests, and Lady Katrin preferred smaller arrangements there.

It turned out that the most senior delegates would stay in the palace, and the top floor was dedicated to their sleeping quarters. Those rooms would require nothing more than fresh bouquets daily. They were not allowed into the prince's private quarters on the western wing of the third floor.

Lady Katrin only said, "His personal staff takes care of all of his needs there."

That was good. Anika had been looking for spots where an assassin could wait in concealment for a moment to strike, and she had found far too many good locations. At least the prince's staff could keep him safe in his quarters. That only left tens of thousands of square feet of palace for them to worry about.

They accessed the roof via another gently curving staircase. The entire roof acted as an enormous balcony, lit by three hundred standing lanterns, flanked by statues representing every Petralist affinity and evergreen topiary in fantastic patterns. They agreed to provide arrangements to add splashes of color.

The rear of the palace faced twelve tiers of the formal gardens that stepped down to a long, still pool, flanked by a shrubbery maze built in eye-twisting patterns. Anika picked out a couple of symbols that she knew were somehow associated with Petralist powers, but she wasn't sure exactly what they meant.

"The gardens are tended by forty full-time gardeners under my direct oversight," Biberach stated proudly. "We require no assistance to maintain them."

Lady Katrin agreed. "Those teams are working well already."

Anika felt immensely relieved. Including the formal gardens in their job would have stretched their talents beyond the breaking point.

When they descended to ground level again, Lady Katrin led them across a long, open patio at the rear of the palace, overlooking the gardens and fountains. A balcony overlooked the patio from the second floor. "Let's focus our outside efforts on this space. Some well-placed shrubbery and flowering plants, I think. Plus, I would love to see a couple of flowering trellises along both ends. That sunset pattern you showcased at the competition would be ideal. I'll leave the other patterns to your judgment."

She then gave them a warm smile. "That's it. Any questions?"

Anika glanced at Sophie, who looked excited and terrified in equal measure.

"I think we've got everything we need for now. Thank you for your time."

"Very well. If you do have any questions, please work through Biberach. I expect you'll work well together, and I hope to see work begin tomorrow. The summit will begin all too soon."

That was an enormous understatement. Even with every able-bodied florist in the city, they'd been hard-pressed to complete the work.

Biberach said grandly, "I'll expect progress reports at the end of each day. If you run into delays, I'll be happy to step in and assist."

"Good," Lady Katrin said. "That's the spirit of cooperation I approve of. Together, we will make the prince proud."

Anika managed a smile, but she was wondering how many rows of hedges she could send Biberach tumbling through. If he thought they'd let him step in and mess with their work, he was in for an abrupt, and painful, jolt of reality.

Sophie curtsied and said, "We appreciate your concern. In fact, it's clear you're already fully engaged with your current duties. Once we complete our work, we'd be happy to consult with you on ways to improve your efficiency and artistry."

"That won't be necessary," he replied quickly, looking insulted.

Excellent.

While they headed back toward the city, Anika tapping granite to manage the heavy chest of coins, Sophie insisted on reviewing their notes immediately, before they forgot everything. She knew every florist, their skills and greatest talents, and began assigning individual florists to each room and each project on their list to best leverage their styles.

She really was the perfect choice to lead the guild. Anika couldn't imagine anyone else possessing her level of mastery of the craft and the players involved. She would have wasted precious time, and probably made incorrect assignments.

Even better, Sophie was already acting as if all of the other girls had already signed up for the job. With her confident leadership, Anika had no doubt they would.

All they needed to do now was to visit them all, procure wagonloads of supplies, and transform the palace into a venue worthy of the summit. Then she'd be positioned to offer any additional services to Ilse and her team.

She hoped the found a spy, and that she'd somehow help identify them. That would be the crowning blossom to her victory wreath.

## 9

## THE SIMPLE JOY OF THROWING
## SOMEONE OUT A WINDOW

Four days later, Anika felt thrilled, but completely exhausted. She'd slept far too little, and talked herself hoarse more than once, but with Sophie's help, she'd recruited all the other florists. Then they'd purchased mountains of supplies through whirlwind shopping trips across Golm and even to Edderitz the day before. Replacement flowers would arrive each morning to freshen up the displays. The logistical challenge had proven enormous, but one of the girls, a seasoned, veteran florist had a knack for management, and Sophie had assigned her to take care of it all.

Now Anika moved through the palace, which had maintained its frantic level of activity all week. The feeling of excitement that infused Reizend was contagious, and it had helped sweep away most of the lingering resentment from the other florists. They'd been caught up in the great floral challenge of their lives, and Anika firmly believed her new guild would win the day.

Of course, the hefty signing bonus the girls had received when they joined the guild had helped a lot too. The nearly unlimited budget they enjoyed guaranteed they had plenty of funds for the work. Lady Katrin demanded perfection, and she was willing to pay handsomely for it.

Anika was nearly finished a circuit of the palace, checking in with each of the florists, many of whom had recruited apprentice helpers from among their family and friends to help with the tedious manual labor under their direction. Sophie was finalizing rules of order and compensation for such assistants, and Anika left those details to her.

As Anika descended the grand staircase, she slowed to inspect Lulu's work. The young florist, who had been the object of affection of the idiot who attacked Anika's booth on competition day, was eagerly wrapping garlands around the baluster.

She still scowled at Anika when she thought Anika wouldn't notice, but she was creating beautiful work, so Anika didn't challenge her on her lingering resentment. Instead, she gave her some encouraging words, convinced the girl would eventually recognize the wonderful opportunity they were all sharing.

She'd last seen Sophie in the grand hall, where she was overseeing work there. The main conference meetings would be held there, and her plans for the floral centerpiece on the main table would far surpass her best work from competition day.

Most of the other assignments she'd made were working out very well. Anika had made a few adjustments, but overall, Sophie managed that aspect of the work efficiently.

Anika was acting as creative director, and she made the rounds of the palace every couple hours. The work was progressing at a phenomenal rate. If the girls kept up that level of intensity, they might just finish in time. Some of the delegates were scheduled to begin arriving the next afternoon, and Anika hoped to have the major arrangements completed by then.

Her contract didn't require completion for two more days, the day prior to the start of the summit, but for any display of force to succeed, it must be ready prior to the arrival of enemy scouts.

Anika focused her personal efforts on the grand entryway, the roof patio, and the ballroom, although other girls were assisting with some of the enormous arrangements. In particular, she needed help with the enormous waterfall of flowers she'd designed to cascade down the eastern wall of the ballroom. She'd purchased five thousand roses of various colors for the effort, and four of the other florists were helping weave the flowers into the supporting wire framework.

The timid young florist, Maud, was one of them, and Anika was glad Sophie hadn't assigned her an entire room to work on her own. The girl could manage basic arrangements, and no doubt her pretty young face helped her sell flowers on the street, but she lacked the ability to comprehend the grand scope of the arrangements they were working on. Still, when given specific instructions, and when overseen by other florists, she worked well enough.

Anika headed back toward the grand entryway. The day before she had completed huge bouquets in standing vases representing each of the nations of the Arishat League.

For the delegation from Althing, who were the political leaders of the Arishat and head delegates for the summit, Anika had constructed a four-tiered arrangement that highlighted five dozen paper flowers that she had fashioned into five-petaled hibiscus using yellowed parchment. Written words covered the visible petals, celebrating the Althins' well-known love for treaties, one dozen for every Arishat nation.

For Ravinder, she'd built a graceful bouquet using ten different zinnia flowers, with varying gentle, paisley shades, surrounded by slender, brown ears of wheat, built over a bed of green kale to celebrate the peaceful nation's bountiful harvests.

Sehrazad, a nation of bold raiders, blowing sands, and fierce independence, deserved a proud arrangement filled with bold blue columbines, red orchids, and rare, golden gladiolus, representing the nation's sandy dunes. Two dozen striking calla lilies made up the bouquet's heart. The trumpet-shaped flowers, with their black hearts, rimmed with purple, stood out beautifully against the others.

Cold, northern Varvakis, with their famous steel weapons and unmatched forging skills, got a bouquet surrounding rare, silver irises and ice-blue orchids.

She wasn't sure if seafarers from the far-southern Tabnit nation would attend the summit, but designed a creative bouquet for them out of multi-colored tulips, woven into the outline of a sailing ship, with tall, drooping snowdrops for masts.

Those beautiful arrangements helped the entryway look great, but it needed to look regal. So she'd woven long chains of flowers and draped them along the walls, then across from several of the tall, fluted columns to the base of the chandelier. She'd finished about half of those chains, and she felt very pleased with the work. The beautiful flower chains created a warm, inviting effect.

Anika stepped through the doorway to the entryway and paused to gape. Her flower chains had fallen to pieces. Some fragments hung limply from the walls, while others still clung to the chandelier like broken dreams. Hundreds of crushed petals covered the floor.

"Thorn and blossoms," Anika muttered as she stepped into the room and inspected the disaster. On rare occasions, she'd had a flower chain break, but never had she seen such a complete failure of her work.

And, of course, at that moment Lady Katrin appeared in the opposite doorway. Anika's heart fell as she watched Lady Katrin's smile fade to surprise, then to outrage.

"What is the meaning of this disaster?" Lady Katrin exclaimed, gesturing around. "The Arishat delegates will arrive tomorrow!"

Anika crossed toward her, cursing her luck that the woman had to arrive at that moment. "I'm so sorry. When I left, everything looked great, but I just got back. I have no idea what happened."

"Well, you'd better get an idea," Lady Katrin declared. "This will never do. Clean up this mess at once. I cannot allow any arrangements that might collapse like this. I thought you knew what you were doing."

"I'll figure out what went wrong, and I'll make the entryway even better than we had planned," Anika promised.

Lady Katrin took a deep breath to settle her nerves. "I will trust that you will. I had thought all was going perfectly until now, but with this disaster, and with reports of problems in the ballroom, I'm starting to worry."

"What reports of problems in the ballroom?" Anika asked quickly. She couldn't afford for that room to suffer a similar catastrophe. In her last visit, the work had been progressing well.

"I don't know yet. I was on my way to visit when I received word that I should check in with you too. I had thought you were inviting me to appreciate your completed work."

A suspicion started forming in Anika's mind. "I didn't send the note. I hadn't expected to finish until tonight, or perhaps tomorrow morning."

"Strange," Lady Katrin said. "I don't have time to run all around the palace all day, you know."

"I'll remind everyone not to bother you with unnecessary reports. In fact, please allow me to deal with the ballroom."

"But you have to deal with this mess."

"I'll deal with that too. That's why I'm here."

"Very well, but see that everything is in order before tonight."

"I promise."

After one more warning look, Lady Katrin headed back into the west wing. Anika sighed, relieved that she hadn't suffered any worse consequences from the poorly timed disaster. She glanced around the flower-strewn grand entryway and picked up one broken segment of her flower chain. It still amazed her that they could have broken. She'd woven the long stems of flowers into a slim, but sturdy vine.

As she studied the broken end of the chain, she noticed that the stems and the vine had all been cleanly cut. They hadn't broken. They'd been sabotaged.

Fury swept through her, and Anika turned a slow circuit, examining the disaster with new understanding. Someone had purposefully destroyed her work. Who would do such a thing?

When she figured that out, they would pay. She was too angry to worry about cleaning up that mess. Instead, she hurried toward the ballroom. What would have happened if there were problems in the ballroom and Lady Katrin witnessed a second mess so soon? Such a double disaster could completely undermine Anika's position with Lady Katrin.

Anika broke into a run.

She ignored startled looks from workers and staff as she ran. Both the entryway and the ballroom were her personal work areas, and any failures there would reflect badly on her more than on the guild or any of the other girls.

A moment later, she rushed through the open doors into the ballroom. Her fears turned out to be true. The huge waterfall of roses, which had been progressing well the last time she checked, was gone. The entire arrangement had been pulled from the wall, and long lines of roses lay in disarray all across the smooth floor.

Her four florists who had been working on the waterfall were clustered together on the far side of the room, facing Biberach, who was shouting at them, shaking an angry finger right under poor Maud's nose. The timid girl was already crying, and looked ready to break into sobs at any second.

The sight of Biberach browbeating her ladies was the last bit of confirmation Anika needed. Fury swept through her and she marched across the ballroom. The florists noticed her coming, and at their relieved smiles, Biberach turned.

When he saw Anika bearing down on him, his arrogant demeanor cracked. He tried to salvage his superiority by demanding haughtily, "Where is Lady Katrin? She needs to see this--"

Anika grabbed him by his perfectly pressed shirt front and hoisted him into the air. His shout of indignant alarm changed into a bleating cry for help as she shook him so violently his teeth clacked together.

Anika pulled the terrified idiot close and demanded, "What is going on here?"

One of the florists, the middle-aged woman who had the booth next to Anika's on competition day, named Els said, "Master Biberach ordered all the roses pulled down."

"Why did you listen to him? He has no authority here?"

"I have authority to correct issues of décor," Biberach argued.

Anika shook him again. "There were no issues. You have no right to interfere unless Lady Katrin decides we're derelict in our duty. You sent for her, didn't you?"

He nodded, gaining courage again. "She should be here any second. And when she sees this mess--"

"A mess that you caused," Anika interrupted.

"I ordered the roses pulled down to demonstrate the flaws in the underlying weave of supporting wire. You cannot hope to achieve the necessary effect using such a simple, unimaginative pattern."

Els threw up her hands and cried, "By Tallan's holy memory, you ordered us to wreck hours of work because you didn't like how we strung the wires?" Even Maud looked ready to strangle him.

Anika was tempted. So very tempted. But she forced herself to walk calmly to the window and carefully pull it open, still carrying Biberach by the front of the shirt.

She told him, "That's the flimsiest excuse I've ever heard."

"It's true," he insisted, pulling uselessly against her hand.

"What's true is that you lack the imagination and intelligence to decorate your dinner plate, let alone the entire palace."

"I have a full staff tending the gardens."

"Right. Your staff does it because you're incompetent."

"I'm twice the decorator you could ever be, you common warrior maiden," Biberach declared, trying to look down his nose at her in a ridiculous attempt at haughty superiority.

Anika laughed in his face. "You can't even grow a beard right, and I doubt you've ever wrestled a girl in your life."

"I do not wrestle. I have served in this palace for years."

"That's why I got the job. You've limited your imagination."

"Unhand me, you brute, or Lady Katrin will hear of this," he ordered her.

Anika's smile faded and she glared. That look had cowed more than one veteran warrior, so it terrified Biberach. She said, "I will make myself clear. You are not to bother any of my girls again. You will not so much as touch a flower anywhere in the palace again. If you do, I will rip that ridiculous excuse for a beard off of your face, then pull out every one of your teeth. If you're lucky, I won't break your fingers."

"You can't," he stammered.

"Try me. Now get out." She wanted to throw him over the formal gardens, but decided to show restraint and use some of that higher level of refinement Sophie was so good at.

So she only tossed him ten feet. They were on the ground floor, and she threw him far enough to clear the flower beds directly under the window. He did manage to flip in the air so he landed on his head, but that was his least useful extremity anyway.

As Biberach staggered to his feet, spitting out dirt, Anika said, "And if you ever attempt to sabotage any of my other arrangements, I'll rip your arms off."

He started, a guilty look on his face, before turning and bolting. Anika swore softly under her breath. She should have ripped out his nose hair, at least. The useless coward had been the one to wreck her entry hall.

Well she'd show him.

After encouraging her girls and helping them get the wire framework back on the wall, she returned to the entry hall and cleaned up her sabotaged flower chains. Her tall bouquet vases were still standing and looked undisturbed. She doubted Biberach would dare smash any of them, but she hesitated to simply re-do the work she'd done before. Those flower chains had proven too easily sabotaged, and the more she thought about it, the more she decided the best revenge on Biberach would be to create something even more spectacular.

She paced the entry hall a few times, studying the high walls, fluted columns, windows, and finally the gilded dome and spectacular chandelier. Then she lay down on the cool tile floor and stared up, trying to immerse herself in the space, imagining this as a defensive bastion where she could spring a surprise assault on an invading force. She'd want to overwhelm them, awe them, remove any hope they ever had of victory.

As she lay there on the cool floor, with the scent of her bouquets creating a pleasant, garden-like aroma throughout the room, she imagined a full squad of Rumbler battle maidens leaping from concealment near every one of those windows and raining down upon an unsuspecting foe.

That was it! Anika rose, grinning. She would recreate that effect, but with flowers. She rushed to the rear of the palace and down to the formal gardens. In their initial tour, she'd spotted a cluster of very tall pole lantern stands, pushed to one corner, as if recently removed from service.

They were still there, and as she inspected them, her excitement grew. They were perfect. Each free-standing pole rose a dozen feet to a junction where a second, thinner pole rose higher still, but curved inward in a graceful angle. They were slender, but strong enough to support heavy lanterns. They'd easily support flowers.

She found a grounds worker, and the man was happy to hear she was taking the poles away. They were often used for garden parties, but Biberach had deemed them unsuitable for the summit. The man even offered to round up a crew to transport them to the entry hall for Anika.

"Thank you," she told him. Then she tapped granite, hefted a pole in each hand, and marched back to the entry hall.

For Anika, creating floral art was as all-engrossing as bash fighting, and she threw herself into a creative frenzy. She spaced the tall poles around the room and secured them to some of the fluted stone columns with iron chains, wrapped in flowers, to ensure no one could push any of them over.

Her plan was to string thin wire between all of the poles, but connecting those wires proved challenging. She did have a free-standing step ladder, but it wasn't quite tall enough. Lowering all the poles to attach the wires before standing them all again did not appeal to her.

Anika was a battle maiden. She wouldn't let something as trivial as high poles interrupt her creative work. So she got a long rope and sent for Sophie.

Sophie arrived a few minutes later, dressed as usual in a bright, flowered dress, although this one was a bit more modest than some of the ones she wore. She carried a small pack with her florist tools, and she frowned at the poles when she stepped into the entry hall. "What happened to garland chains?"

"Biberach sabotaged them. I've moved on."

"You didn't kill him, did you?" Sophie asked, glancing around, as if expecting to see the annoying official stuffed into a vase somewhere nearby.

"Not yet. I caught him giving our girls problems in the ballroom. We had a few words," Anika said simply.

Surprisingly, that didn't look like it eased Sophie's worries. "You usually speak with your fists, Anika."

"Well, I did throw him out a window," Anika admitted.

At Sophie's appalled look, she quickly added, "It was a first-floor window, and it was open. I made sure he landed in soft dirt."

"We can't go around beating up the palace staff," Sophie warned.

"And he can't go around undermining our work. Watch out for him. He's a small-minded man, filled with jealousy. I scared him, but I don't know if it's enough to keep him from causing more trouble."

"Is that why you sent for me, so we can plot ways to remove him for good?" Sophie asked. The idea seemed to worry and excite her in equal measure. She'd definitely make a good guild matron.

"No. I need help." Anika gestured at the high poles.

"Really?" Sophie asked, looking like she liked hearing that from Anika.

"Sure." Anika picked up the rope and handed it to Sophie.

"Um, what am I supposed to do with this?" Sophie's smile faded.

Anika pointed up at the chandelier high overhead. "I need you to tie the rope through the support chain. I'll use the rope to access the high poles."

Sophie considered the high chandelier nervously. "Exactly how am I supposed to do that?"

"Simple." Anika lifted her by her foot, just as she had when they first arrived in the palace. Sophie adjusted easily this time, standing balanced on Anika's hand. "I'm going to throw you up there."

"Maybe we can think of a better way," Sophie suggested.

"Don't worry. When you're done, jump. I'll catch you," Anika promised.

Instead of protesting again, Sophie said, "All right. I can do that, but I won't need to jump."

"Why not?"

Sophie drew some gloves and a leather leg wrap out of her bag. She slid her right foot into the leg brace, which wrapped her from ankle almost up to her knee, then donned the thick gloves. Most of the florists used gloves like that when processing thorny flowers.

"What is that leg brace?" Anika asked.

"Throw me, and I'll show you."

Intrigued, Anika threw Sophie. Carefully. She didn't want to snap her legs or give her whiplash. Anika was one of the best throwers in her squad. She regularly threw weights far heavier than one skinny florist a lot higher than that chandelier.

Sophie laughed as she soared high into the air. Anika smiled in satisfaction as Sophie rose just high enough to reach the top of the chandelier. With a dancer's grace, she slipped one foot into the large, golden ring that connected the chandelier to the heavy support chain.

It took only a moment to tie off the rope. Anika gave it an experimental tug, and shouted, "Feels good. You can jump any time."

"I told you, I have a better idea," Sophie called back down.

Grasping the rope in her gloved hands, she jumped away from the chandelier and began to slide downward. As Sophie descended, she wrapped the rope around her leather-wrapped leg and used that extra leverage to slow her slide.

She descended in graceful slow motion and started executing a series of aerial acrobatic maneuvers. It was like watching her dance down the rope. She leaned and twirled and spun, sometimes flinging out one hand and her free leg to spin herself. Once, she even wrapped the rope around her waist and leaned back, both hands extended, as if she was flying upside down.

Anika gaped. She'd never seen anything like it. Sophie dropped to the floor nearby, breathing a bit heavily from the exertion, but grinning as happily as Anika had ever seen her.

"Where did you learn to do that?" Anika asked.

"I told you I was a dancer. I spent a year studying aerial dancing in Edderitz when I was still a girl. Of course, there we used smoother cloth. That rope hurts even through the leather wrap, but I couldn't help it. I haven't had an excuse to aerial dance in months."

"It looked like a lot of fun," Anika admitted. She'd never imagined dancing on a rope. She wondered if there were rope-dance wrestling techniques she could learn. Would she ever find a man able to wrestle her on a rope, twenty feet in the air? The very thought made her pulse race.

"Maybe I'll teach you a little some time," Sophie offered.

"That would be fun. But let's finish our work first."

"I'll check on the other girls on my way back to the great hall," Sophie offered.

After she left, Anika got to work. With granite-enhanced strength, she scampered up the rope and, pushing herself from pole to pole, attached the wires. Some she ran between the high tops, a full twenty feet in the air. Others she connected from top sections down to the lower junctions, a mere dozen feet above the floor, creating a multi-level web of invisible wires.

Then the fun really started. Anika tied small clusters of flowers together, then draped those little clusters off of the wires at varying heights. The effect produced a sense of a raining flowers, suspended in mid-fall overhead.

After two hours, she'd finished about a third of the

work, and when she paused for a drink of water, she decided she loved it. That flowered rain would be one of her signature works. Not only would the impressive display help separate her work, and the work of her guild, from all who had come before, but it would send Biberach into a fit of jealousy.

If he ever touched another of her flowers, she'd rip off every one of his fingers. Politely.

## 10

## POMP AND CIRCUMSTANCE, AND POISON

A couple days later, Anika stood at the edge of the great hall near a staff entrance concealed behind a ten-foot-tall statue of a Wingrunner in a fully-fracked sprint. Sophie stood beside her, while a dozen other staff members, most in the blue and silver of Prince Theodor's colors, flanked her, all standing at attention and trying to look invisible. The other florists were in position in various rooms of the palace to watch over the decorations.

The summit was beginning with a great deal of pomp and ceremony. The hall was full to bursting with people, all focused on the long table where Crown Prince Theodor presided. The large chandelier that hung above the table glowed with warm golden light, generated by a Solas. It filled the room with soft illumination, driving back the shadows of the deepening twilight outside.

The prince was dressed in a formal uniform of Grandurian deep blue, trimmed in crimson. His thick, blond hair was longer than military standard, and his blue eyes seemed to twinkle as he spoke in his rich voice, enhanced by quartzite.

"Welcome to my home, friends and neighbors. I extend our hospitality and offer of continuing friendship. We face trying times, but together I am confident we can weather any storm."

His voice filled the room in a way only a Longseer's could. It contained inflections not possible for unenhanced voices, and the prince had clearly trained hard in every nuance of his tertiary power. As he continued, speaking of fostering greater friendship between Granadure and the member states of the Arishat League, Anika felt her heart stirring with patriotic pride and with feelings of optimism about the summit.

Beside Anika, Sophie sighed and whispered, "I could listen to him. That voice is better than the finest flower nectar."

Anika had never actually tried nectar. She whispered back, "Don't get distracted."

She scanned the room, her training as a battle maiden reinforced by her work as the palace's main florist. She saw no active threats from any of the visitors. More importantly, she spotted no flaws in Sophie's work. The flowers looked spectacular.

The long table that filled the center of the room held the delegates and their aids from all five Arishat nations, along with half a dozen of the prince's chief advisors and military leaders. Even then the table did not seem crowded.

But Anika's eyes went to the glorious floral centerpiece. Sophie and her team had produced the finest work of their careers. They'd crafted a delicately beautiful centerpiece that flowed across the table like a vibrant carpet of blues and whites, extending over the sides and cascading down both sides to the floor.

"That centerpiece is perfect," she whispered.

Sophie allowed a little smile, and Anika was happy to

see it. Sophie had been so stressed about that centerpiece, Anika had worried she'd suffer a breakdown. When she'd visited the day before, she'd found Sophie agonizing over the mostly-completed centerpiece.

"What's wrong?" she'd asked.

"It needs something more," Sophie had cried. "But I don't have anything else."

Luckily, Lady Katrin had provided the perfect solution. She'd swept into the hall, followed by workers carrying several wooden crates. Under her direction, they'd revealed the breathtaking contents.

"Where did you get those?" Sophie had breathed as she extracted a delicate silver nebel flower.

"From the Valeska River, of course," Lady Katrin had laughed. The silvery flowers grew only there, on the borders of the great Lake Pyasino.

"And lebhaft roses," Anika exclaimed as she examined another crate. The rare, silver-white flowers were found only in the remote, high meadows of northwest Granadure, bordering Ravinder.

Those crates probably cost her half again as much as the entire amount she'd allocated for decorating the rest of the Reizend for the summit.

Lady Katrin had looked immensely pleased that they understood the enormous value of those flowers. She had sniffed the gentle, pleasant scent of the lebhaft rose and smiled with satisfaction. "Reizend and the prince both deserve the very best. I trust that with these additions to your stores, you can complete your work and that you will utilize them to their best effect."

"Oh, yes!" Sophie exclaimed, so filled with excitement she'd started bouncing on her toes with eagerness to get to work.

With those flowers as the crown jewels of the arrangement, Sophie had finished the project in less than an hour. Those silver flowers perfectly offset the deep blues of the irises, delphinium, and morning glory.

Now as Anika surveyed the result, she felt a deep sense of pride for her guild. That arrangement perfectly set the tone for the rest of the room and made an exquisite backdrop against which the colorful outfits of the Arishat delegates could shine.

Victory had never felt so good. Lady Katrin was thrilled by the beautiful decorations, and the florists were ecstatic with success. Anika had authorized Sophie to pay them all another portion of their shares, and any lingering hesitation about the new guild seemed to be melting.

Anika allowed herself a moment to feel confident. She'd set out to take the floral community by storm, but she'd done so much more. She'd united them into a special-forces floral strike force that had transformed Reizend in a matter of days.

Let the diplomats talk for days. To them, her contribution might seem small, but within the sphere of her influence, she was victor. She owned the florist guild, and even though Sophie was already beginning to accept more and more responsibility over it, everyone knew the victory belonged to her.

Anika glanced around the room again while the prince continued his opening remarks. She had hoped to spot her brother, or Ilse. They were there somewhere, proving a covert additional level of security, but she did not see them. They had not shared any more intelligence about the potential threat of a spy, so maybe the report had been a false alarm.

So Anika tried to soak up as much intelligence as possible regarding the Arishat League. When Captain Ilse accepted her into the special clandestine team, some of their missions might take them into the Arishat nations, so the more Anika understood about them, the better.

Anika had not yet interacted with any of them. The Althin delegate, who chaired the Arishat League caucus, was a middle-aged woman whose thick hair was actually brown instead of the usual white-blonde of most of her aides, tied in a tight bun. She wore a beautiful, emerald green gown with flowing skirt and a fitted bodice covered in gold brocade.

Her retinue seemed to enjoy bright colors and woolen fabrics. They all carried thick, leather bags stuffed to overflowing with papers, parchments, and scrolls. The Althin love of treaties was well known. She hoped the prince kept his signing quill locked up in his safe.

The Varvakan delegation sat next, led by a full general. They dressed in black and brown, preferring furs, thick leather, and gleaming steel. Their swarthy skin, full beards, and burly, military bearing drew the gaze of most of the prince's soldiers stationed around the room. If any fighting started, the Varvakans would prove the deadliest threats.

All foreigners had been required to surrender long weapons, with the exception of the delegates themselves. The general wore a heavy broadsword and dagger at his belt, but Anika wasn't worried he'd leap up and murder the prince. Prince Theodor was a Rumbler in his primary affinity. No doubt he'd absorbed a little granite prior to the start of the summit. Even if trouble started, the Varvakans' weapons would avail little against stone-hardened skin and superhuman strength.

Anika would have expected the general might have felt a bit uneasy entering the palace where he could not hope to win a fight, but he and all his retinue looked eager. They didn't look like a trusting lot, so she wondered at their attitude. Might they feel they could win significant advantage during the summit? She simply didn't know enough to guess.

The Sehrazad delegate sat on the opposite side of the table, head wrapped in a cloth turban, clothed in flowing white robes, a wide-bladed scimitar at his belt. His skin was even darker than the Varvakans, and he surveyed the room with a black-eyed stare over a prominent nose and equally prominent scowl. He didn't pretend to like visiting Granadure, but he too listened attentively to the prince's words and also seemed eager for the summit to get underway.

His aides at the table were strong-looking men, dressed similarly in white or gray robes. The rest of his party, hovering behind, included a dozen women whose faces were concealed behind gauzy veils. No doubt many Grandurian men found them mysterious and alluring, but Anika found it annoying. It was harder to read a potential threat when they concealed so much of their expression.

The delegate from Ravinder seemed downright plain compared to the others. Ravinder was a nation of farmers and traders, and their delegation reflected that. The leader was a woman in rich clothing, cut more sensibly than the Althins. Her retinue tended to prefer pastel colors and sensible shoes.

Anika felt pleased that she'd gotten so much right with her floral vases in the entryway. Had the delegates even noticed those flowers? Would they understand the effort she put into making them special?

It didn't matter, really. Anika knew, and no doubt Captain Ilse would notice. Anika doubted that woman missed anything.

The last group at the table was a delegation all the way from Tabnit, the mysterious lands far to the south, beyond the Sea of Olcan. She'd never met anyone from Tabnit before, and she hoped to find a chance to speak with them, maybe find out how well they wrestled.

The head delegate wore a rich, purple doublet and a short, flaring cape of deep burgundy. His pants were simple, brown canvas, tucked into tall leather boots with soft uppers, rolled down to just above the calf. An enormous, plumed hat sat on the table in front of him. His tanned skin and weathered face suggested a life spent outdoors. He wore his black hair long, nearly to shoulder length, with a goatee and long, waxed mustache. The men of his retinue dressed in similar exotic fashion. The women wore long dresses and preferred gauzy scarves with intricate, woven patterns.

Anika took her time surveying the delegates' retinues. She doubted the delegates would personally get involved in any treachery. They would prefer to direct any nefarious activities and leave the dirty work to their staff. She scanned the crowds, looking for any hint that might suggest they were the kind of unscrupulous, black-hearted swine who might steal flowers out of a perfect arrangement.

The problem was, she wasn't sure how to read the foreigners. Did their expressions mean the same in their countries as it did in Granadure? The summit was supposed to be a wonderful relationship-building experience. She doubted the delegates would openly risk that ultimate objective, but didn't doubt they had ulterior motives.

The prince spoke for another five minutes, but the time passed quickly with his sonorous voice caressing their ears. When he fell silent, Anika joined in the enthusiastic applause. That man sure knew how to work a crowd, and by all outward appearances, he'd won everyone over.

The Althing delegate, Lady Briel, rose. She spoke Grandurian with almost no accent, and seemed accustomed to wielding power. She did not look intimidated by the crowds or by the challenge of following the prince's impressive speech.

"Thank you for your generous hospitality. We of the Arishat League join enthusiastically with you in exploring new ways to strengthen ties and combine efforts to step confidently into the future. Together we can overcome any obstacle and build pathways to mutual success."

While the crowds cheered again, Anika took the opportunity to slip from the room. The woman looked ready to speak for half an hour, and no doubt every other delegate would take a turn to share long, pompous, prepared remarks. Anika felt grateful she wasn't stationed as a guard, watching over the event, trying to remain focused and alert, despite the mind-numbing monologuing that would surely ensue.

She much preferred slipping through the palace, checking the status of the decorations in the other rooms and verifying her girls remained alert. The entire guild was on hand to make sure everything looked perfect for the first-day opening ceremonies.

Sophie caught up with her as she moved down the east wing. Sophie looked thrilled with the singular opportunity to move about the palace during the summit. She was dressed like all the florists in a simple, white linen dress with a blue sash.

"How is everything?" She asked Anika.

"All good down this wing. Why don't you head up to the second floor? One of the flower chains had seemed a bit weak earlier."

"Good idea. I'll make sure it didn't give way."

"Excellent. I'll check the back patio," Anika decided.

The patio looked exquisite against the backdrop of the soft twilight, so Anika headed up to the roof. The space now felt like a long garden patio, with flowering plants in place between the imposing statues, and with trellises covered in flowering vines arcing overhead every fifty feet.

Anika paced the length of the roof, feeling satisfied. Everything looked great. A reception would take place later in the evening so the back patio and the roof would most likely see a great deal of use.

The far western end of the roof, directly over the prince's quarters was blocked by a pair of guards. Anika nodded in approval at their alert postures and headed back toward the stairs. After a hundred feet, she stopped.

A nearby bush, trimmed in a simple, spiral pattern, was wrapped in a beautiful wreath that burst with colors from dozens of different flowers. Everything about the bush and the wreath looked perfectly in order, except for one strange grouping of white roses near the bottom.

Frowning, Anika drew closer and crouched for a better look. Whoever had woven that wreath had done an artful job. It didn't make sense that they'd leave a clump of white like that. It broke up the pattern. Anika doubted anyone but a florist would notice the subtle mistake, but it was the first such sloppy mistake she'd seen in all her review of her girls' work.

Anika leaned closer and fingered the odd grouping of white roses. At her touch, two of them fell right out of the arrangement.

Surprised, she caught them and noted their short stems. The flowers hadn't been woven in with the others, but placed onto the wreath after it was completed. Strange.

A broken stem ended at the spot where the flowers had fallen, as if someone had plucked another flower away to make room for them. Anika reached out to touch the blank vine there and was startled to feel parchment crinkling under her finger.

Upon closer scrutiny, she found a narrow piece of

parchment wrapped around the vine. The paper was colored in bands of muted green and brown that camouflaged it against the backdrop of shadows cast by the flowers.

Intrigued, she unwrapped the parchment and turned it over.

The other side was uncolored, with a short message written in a clean hand.

*The plan is in motion. We will proceed.*
*I have the poison you requested.*

## 11

## NEED SUBTLE? CALL A BASH FIGHTER

Ten minutes later, Anika met with her brother and with Captain Ilse in a shadowed corner of the back patio. The opening ceremony of the summit would soon conclude. Probably. The prince and the delegates would retire to another long hall where a sumptuous feast was prepared for them and all their retinues.

The feasting would undoubtedly last for hours, and only then would the crowds disperse out to the patio and the rooftop. That meant that the three of them stood alone. No one could approach to eavesdrop without their notice, and Ilse had ordered one of the Longseers from the Crusher squad to establish a buffer perimeter against the unlikely event of quartzite long-distance listening.

Petralists were rare in the Arishat League, but they'd occasionally hired Obrioner mercenaries. If there really was an Obrioner spy attempting to infiltrate the summit, they would be even more likely to possess the useful tertiary ability.

"You're certain you didn't overlook anything else?" Ilse asked.

She spoke softly, despite the rushing wind that whistled around them, ten feet out on every side. The Longseer was skilled at the tricky air manipulation that blocked their words from any listeners.

Anika appreciated the fact that the captain didn't waste time asking her to repeat what she had already shared. Ilse believed her report, and that confidence made Anika stand tall with pride.

"That was the entire message. I saw nothing else, but did not take the time to search every branch for more camouflaged messages. I was too eager to interview the guards posted above the prince's quarters to see if they'd noticed anyone linger in that area."

"That would have been too easy," Erich said with a frown.

He too was taking the message seriously. He hadn't teased her about her flowers once, which she appreciated. But he hadn't complimented them yet, either, and that annoyed her. He couldn't afford to miss opportunities to demonstrate to Captain Ilse that he noticed important things.

"I would have been amazed if whoever went through all the trouble of concealing this note so well had made such an amateurish blunder," Ilse agreed.

"Do you think it's the spy you heard reports about?" Anika asked.

"Perhaps, but it is not the only possibility. Clandestine communications during a summit are not unusual. Poison is."

"Do you want me to warn the prince's guard?" Erich asked.

Ilse shook her head. "They're already on high alert, and protocols are in place to guard the prince against poison."

"Do you have any idea who the target is?" Anika asked.

"The prince, probably," Erich offered.

Captain Ilse considered that. "Again, perhaps. If the message was from a spy, they may well hope to poison Prince Theodor. Depends on their overall mission. Are they here to assassinate, or to disrupt? Are their orders merely to observe, or to actively attempt sabotage?"

She hesitated and studied them for a moment. "There is another possibility we must consider. Whoever our mystery poisoner is, they may be here to steal the secret of the new weakening agent."

Anika gasped. "So it's true?"

She'd heard rumors of a remarkable new substance that, if ingested by granite Petralists, not only blocked their granite strength, but left them weaker than a wilted dandelion.

She hadn't wanted to believe the rumors. Sure, such an agent could act as a powerful new weapon against Obrion. But if their enemies ever learned the secret, they could turn it back against Granadure with equally devastating effects.

If Obrion gained that secret, it might give them the confidence to launch an invasion into Granadure. They'd been acting increasingly aggressive in recent months. War was coming. It was just a matter of when.

Ilse said, "It is true. The secret is closely guarded by General Wolfram, but one of his staff was caught just last month trying to smuggle some of the powder out of the testing facility. I haven't heard why, but it's possible Obrion has heard of it. Unfortunately, the Arishat League definitely has."

Erich frowned, looking deeply disturbed by the news. His strength was his defining characteristic. If someone could rob him of that, it would be like stealing his soul.

Would Anika handle such a debilitating disaster any better?

"That's why the delegates seemed so eager, isn't it?" Anika asked.

"I'm glad you noticed that. I'm not involved in the prince's counseling sessions, but I've heard rumors that the Arishat delegates will push for some kind of demonstration during the summit."

"Prince Theodor wouldn't share it with them, would he?" Erich demanded. He looked like he'd consider tearing Reizend apart before allowing the secret to become general knowledge. As long as he didn't mess with her flowers.

"Some kind of demonstration may be required. It would prove the truth of the claim, bolster Granadure's position against increasing Obrioner aggression, and strengthen his negotiating position here during the summit."

"But we can't let a spy get their hands on it," Anika objected.

"No, we cannot. We must catch whoever the mystery poisoner is, but we must tread cautiously."

"Why?" Erich asked.

"Because clearly there's not just a single conspirator. The note suggests a plot, but we don't know if it's between foreigners, or if there's a local insider working with them."

"Traitors," Anika hissed. She hated the very thought of anyone betraying their nation, and by heiderkraut, she'd rip their arms off if she ever found them.

"I doubt they see themselves as such," Ilse said. "Prince Theodor has vocal opponents. Some are here in attendance. Lord Ramwold, for example. He feels we should keep our distance from the Arishat League."

Anika had heard Lord Ramwold's public position. He felt that the Arishat League was taking advantage of Granadure and needed to invest more in the relationship. He called for more trade and more meaningful commitment to partnering with Granadure.

Erich asked, "So what do we do?"

"We don't jump to conclusions," Ilse said. "There may be a spy. There may be intrigue from the Arishat League. There may be Grandurian opponents of the prince seeking to use the summit against him, but blame the foreigners."

Erich said, "We could compare the note to other samples of writing from attendees."

That was a pretty good idea. Since when did Erich start thinking on his own?

Ilse said, "Perhaps, but that little note is not nearly enough proof to convict anyone. We don't even have the note."

"I could go fetch it," Anika offered. She'd replaced the note and flowers exactly as she'd found them, hoping to return with reinforcements to catch the next conspirator when they tried to take it.

"It could be gone by the time we return for it. Even if we do get it, that note alone is not enough proof. The conspirators could claim Anika invented the story and wrote the note herself, or that someone else forged it."

"Do you really think we might be dealing with a domestic conspiracy?" Anika asked. She found it hard to believe anyone would disagree over policy to such deadly, deceitful levels.

"It's impossible to say at this point. Lord Ramwold and Lord Leuthold might benefit most from some disaster befalling the prince. They're the senior court officials after Prince Theodor, but they're already leading most of the direct negotiations. From all reports, they're very effective at it, so I'd be surprised if they would risk their position. Lesser officials in attendance wouldn't win as much advantage unless they also targeted those two, so again, it makes no sense."

"So you're thinking maybe it's not a local," Anika said.

"I simply don't know, but we'll find out who they mean to poison, and stop them."

Erich shrugged. "That's why you dispatched the other Longseer and a squad of Rumblers to monitor the note. They'll catch whoever goes to fetch it."

"Let us assume so. In the meantime, we support the prince's guard in keeping him safe. Good work, Anika. Notify me if you identify any other leads."

"Yes, ma'am." Anika saluted, feeling thrilled. Ilse was already treating her like a team member. She already had a lot to do in keeping the decorations in perfect condition and monitoring the other florists, with Sophie's help. But helping to collar a foreign spy would definitely secure her place in Ilse's company.

"What are we authorized to do?" Erich asked.

"Whatever it takes to keep the prince and the delegates safe."

When he began to grin Ilse added in a warning tone, "But the goal is to minimize damage and interruption."

Erich looked so disappointed, Anika added, "We wouldn't get a bash fight anyway, so trying to be subtle isn't all bad."

"Subtle is not my greatest strength," Erich admitted ruefully.

Ilse and Anika both grinned in silent laughter at the enormous understatement.

1 2

## UNLEASH THE FLORISTS!

Anika yearned to climb back to the roof and position herself with the squad watching that shrub, but forced herself to stay away. With a Longseer monitoring the location from the far end of the roof, they'd know the instant someone dislodged that flower and unwrapped the dangerous note. The Crushers stationed around the roof would close in and subdue the conspirator.

They knew their job, but Anika was tempted to remind them not to smash any of her flowers. They'd get the fun of taking down the conspirator, but she and her girls would have to clean up the mess, and they'd be blamed if any of the delegates or, Tallan forbid, the prince himself, noticed anything amiss.

It also rankled to think that someone else would make the capture. Anika was the one who had found the note, so she should get that victory.

Captain Ilse's orders were clear, though, so Anika prowled the rest of the palace, feeling restless and imagining assassins lurking in every shadow.

"Anika, is something wrong?"

She paused in the ornate first floor hall and turned to find Sophie approaching.

Sophie asked, "What went wrong?"

"Nothing," Anika assured her.

"I noticed you scowling when you passed the music room. Did one of the arrangements fail? Did that trellis on the patio catch fire? I knew it was too close to that lantern."

"It's nothing like that," Anika said, raising a calming hand, "Although you're right about that trellis. Maybe we should move it over a bit."

In that moment, Anika realized she was being foolish, moping that Erich got to hunt a spy with Ilse while she minded the flowers. No one else could do her job, but over a hundred soldiers would be helping Erich.

"Then what?" Sophie demanded.

Anika realized that she'd undervalued her position. Only her knowledge of flowers and her attention to detail had identified that concealed note. No one else, no matter how skilled in battle or identifying concealed weapons, or sniffing out poisons would have ever found that note.

Their clever enemy had not anticipated the florists.

Anika held a secret trump card that not even the resourceful Captain Ilse commanded.

She gripped Sophie's shoulder and, after glancing both ways to ensure they were alone in the long hallway, said softly, "There is potentially fatal intrigue already afoot and we've been recruited to help ferret out a possible enemy spy."

Sophie's eyes widened in surprise and she leaned closer to ask in a breathless whisper. "What happened? What spy?"

"We don't know who yet. They may be concealed among the Arishat delegations, or among the temporary staff brought in for the summit." She didn't add they might be important Grandurian officials.

Sophie glanced around nervously. "Tallan preserve us. What are we going to do?"

"We're going to let the guards and the security forces do their jobs while we do ours."

"I thought you said we're getting recruited to help."

"We are. The enemy has already tried to pass a note to other conspirators." Anika explained about the out-of-place flowers and the camouflaged note.

As she talked, Sophie nodded thoughtfully. She looked both frightened and thrilled at the same time.

Anika concluded, "So you and I are going to quietly circulate among the other girls. Tell them to continue checking on every floral arrangement and look for anything out of place. If they see anything, report it to me immediately. I'll investigate. If we keep a sharp lookout, we may be able to provide critical information for the security team to identify the spies."

Sophie eagerly agreed to the plan, and headed to the second floor to start spreading the word. Anika watched her hurry away with a sense of deep satisfaction, then turned and continued down the long hallway. She'd recruit all the other girls on the first floor. With the guild engaged in the hunt, they'd ferret out the secret enemy before dawn.

Over the next hour, she and Sophie quietly spoke with all of the florists. As a group, they spent the next two hours scouring Reizend for any other secret notes, but found nothing. The feasting lasted the entire time, followed by hours more of quiet conversation as the delegations from the various nations mingled and chatted with the many aides and officers and officials from the prince's retinue.

As the night grew late, Anika found Captain Ilse

prowling one of the lower halls and reported their lack of progress.

"Good work. Keep up the search."

"How late will these meetings last?" Anika asked. Some of the girls were growing noticeably tired.

"Some of the delegates may keep meeting until near dawn. These types of face-to-face meetings are rare, and much productive negotiating happens during these informal, late-night chats. It's also a perfect opportunity for conspirators to meet and make plans without anyone noticing."

"Unless the prince has Longseers listening," Anika said.

"Rules of the summit prevent Petralist eavesdropping, but no doubt they would use coded phrases, just in case."

"Any word from the rooftop team?" Anika couldn't help inquiring.

Ilse shook her head. "They are still monitoring the shrub. No one approached the concealed message."

"I hope they do."

If they were Arishat League members, making their nefarious plans public would certainly strengthen the prince's negotiating position. If they were Obrioner spies, that would help motivate the parties to negotiate against that common enemy. She only hoped they weren't Grandurian. Such a public embarrassment might weaken the prince's position.

As midnight came and went, she made another round of the girls. None of them had noticed any other aberrations, although Anika wondered how disciplined they'd remained in watching flowers instead of the many handsome foreigners. Some of the girls looked decidedly distracted and giggled together about particularly interesting men.

They had all been given beds in a crowded servants' bunkhouse situated on the grounds so they could return to work early the following morning. Twenty-nine florists had joined the guild so far, plus Anika and Sophie, so when they headed for bed an hour after midnight, they filled an entire floor of the bunkhouse. Most of them looked tired, but happy.

That should make Anika feel happy too, but she retired to bed a bit frustrated. She preferred meeting an enemy in the open, pitting her strength against theirs. Creeping through the shadows, playing cat-and-mouse through the Reizend was annoying. As she faded off to sleep, she decided she'd find the conspirators the next day for sure.

In the morning, after a quick breakfast, she led her florists back into position. The girls scattered to their posts to freshen up the displays, swap out any wilting blossoms, and prepare for another long day.

Captain Ilse summoned Anika to a tiny office near the kitchens that she'd commandeered. A frown tugged down the corners of her mouth and she said without preamble, "I checked the bush this morning. The note is gone."

"What? How? Wasn't someone monitoring it all night?" Anika exclaimed.

"They were. Guards remained in position over the prince's wing all night, and a Longseer listened throughout the night from down in the formal gardens. They heard nothing."

Anika frowned. The guards should have noticed anyone moving around after the rest of the guests went to bed. The Longseer might not have had a clear line of sight from down in the formal gardens up to the rooftop, but at only a few hundred yards away, they should have easily heard footsteps on the roof. Certainly they would have noticed the crinkle of parchment unwrapping from the vine.

"The note was still there when everyone went to bed?" she asked.

"Yes."

"So how could they do it without anyone noticing? Who could do that?"

"That's the question I've been pondering. I cannot imagine a non-Petralist succeeding."

Anika breathed in long and slow, considering the ramifications of that. "So we really are dealing with an Obrioner spy, but who are they communicating with?"

"It is possible the Arishat League hired a mercenary to work for them." Ilse's expression turned downright grave. "Or, what if they brought a Mhortair, concealed among their delegations?"

"Would they dare bring in an Assassin?" Anika breathed. She hadn't considered the deadly Mhortair, hadn't believed the Arishat would take such a monumental risk.

Concealed somewhere among the Arishat League, the Mhortair were supposed to possess unmatched abilities at infiltration, stealth, and dealing death. Most of what Anika had heard were rumors and legend. She couldn't remember ever hearing any confirmed reports of clashes with the Mhortair. To her knowledge, none of them had even been captured alive, and only on extremely rare occasions were any ever killed.

They were strictly outlawed in Granadure and would be executed on sight. If the Arishat delegations had smuggled a Mhortair into the prince's palace for the summit, and if that Mhortair assassin was captured, the alliance everyone claimed to want would collapse.

"Even a skilled Obrioner Pathfinder would find it difficult to sneak past an attentive, listening Longseer without alerting them."

Anika opened her mouth to ask the question that statement begged, but she couldn't bring herself to speak the words.

Ilse seemed to read her mind. "The Longseer did remain attentive all night. Her three companions all testified to that fact."

Anika breathed a sigh of relief. She hadn't wanted to implicate another soldier, and she was glad Captain Ilse had already checked that possibility. Such a lapse was rare, and any soldier who fell asleep while on duty protecting the prince would face severe reprimand.

Still, that would be preferable to dealing with a Mhortair.

"So what do we do now?" Anika asked.

"You've already recruited your girls?"

"I have." Anika couldn't hide her surprise. She'd thought that brilliant stroke of genius was her little secret.

"I knew I could count on you to see the advantage of confiding in your guild and to take the initiative to bring them into the hunt. Everything is a test, Anika. Don't forget that."

"I won't," Anika assured her, relieved and pleased with herself that she'd passed that test. Were there other tests Ilse had set for her that she hadn't recognized yet?

"Good. Are you sure you can trust them all?"

Anika wanted to immediately declare that of course she did, but how well did she know her guild members? She considered the question for a few seconds before saying, "I trust Sophie, and she knows the girls, and did not express any concerns. But I can double-check with her."

"Very well. And make sure to instill upon your girls the need for strict confidence. I know the risk is small, but I do not want them blabbing to the wrong person that they're looking for concealed notes. The enemy knew to use extreme caution last night, so they may already know we're on the hunt."

"I'll take care of it."

"They may be the resource that this clever enemy fails to account for. Report any new findings to me. Good hunting."

Anika left with renewed optimism and moved through the palace, checking in with every florist, reminding them to keep their decorations at the highest level of perfection. She shared Captain Ilse's charge of secrecy with them too.

Most of them took the responsibility seriously, but a couple looked like they saw the secret mission as a way to impress good-looking potential amours. Lulu, in particular, seemed eager to find a way to catch the eye of one of the pale-haired Althins.

So Anika tapped a bit of granite, shifting to perfectly sculpted lines, her skin taking on a rose hue. Using her drill sergeant voice, she warned, "Don't treat this mission lightly. If your loose lips result in the prince getting injured, you will be held responsible for your actions."

Lulu retreated, looking nervous, but also angry. "I'll do my duty. You don't have to threaten me."

"I want to make it clear that we're not playing games."

"Life is a game," Lulu shot back. "I'm a poor girl, with few prospects. So I need to make my play when I see my chance."

"You're part of something bigger now," Anika reminded her. Lulu had a point, but they weren't just selling flowers on street corners any more. "You have responsibilities to your guild and to your prince."

Lulu grunted, frowning. "So the guild is already imposing restrictions and trying to control my life? I thought you promised you wouldn't do that."

Anika released granite, feeling frustrated. She spoke

more softly. "I'm not trying to control you. We've been asked to help, so I need to know you will, or I need you to walk out the door and not return."

When Lulu crossed her arms, her jaw set stubbornly, Anika added, "The guild is giving you much. You have work, good pay, and access to witness this summit. It's not a lot to ask that you help keep an eye out for enemies of our nation, is it?"

"I suppose not," Lulu admitted, still looking a bit sullen.

Anika felt relieved. She hadn't wanted to force any of the girls out. "Thank you."

She worried about Lulu and the few other girls who seemed to not understand the importance of their duty, but in her rounds, she saw none of them doing anything inappropriate. The day progressed slowly, and despite Anika's attempts to remain ever-vigilant, she had to admit the search was proving rather boring. The delegates spent the bulk of the day in closed-door meetings, negotiating updated terms of their existing alliance.

As Ilse had feared, the Arishat delegations possessed knowledge of the weakening agent, and as they enjoyed a sumptuous luncheon feast, that topic became a central issue.

Anika heard about the intense negotiations second-hand from Erich, who attended many of them as a member of the security team. The afternoon session was derailed for over an hour as the delegates hotly debated dozens of proposals that included various degrees of inclusion of that critical weakening agent as a key element.

"The Arishat delegates are desperate to get their hands on that secret," Erich told her.

"The prince won't give it to them, will he?" Anika asked.

"He's very careful in his responses. The man is an excellent politician."

That meant he probably drove Erich insane with his carefully worded responses.

Erich sighed. "If only the man would flat out tell them it won't happen. We'd save days of argument. At least he's given Lord Ramwold more leeway to speak. He's stated that position for him. Lord Leuthold plays the opposite approach, but his position seems to be weakening. They actually work well together, even though I've heard they detest each other personally."

"It still bothers me to think so many potential conspirators have such close access to the prince."

"How could we prevent it? We don't have the note, or any credible suspicions of who is involved. Don't worry, little sister, we're keeping an eye on all the nobles and their retinues. The arguments are keeping them busy, and maybe Lord Ramwold's harder line will make the secret conspirators angry enough to make a mistake."

"Wow. You're actually paying attention," Anika teased.

"It's interesting when I imagine that any second, one of the delegates might reach for a knife."

Anika laughed fondly at him. "You'd love a chance to throw that Varvakan general out one of those huge windows."

Erich nodded with a grin.

"Better to find the poisoner."

"Especially if they resist arrest," Erich agreed.

"What do you think they'll decide?" Anika asked. Erich was no politician, but she was impressed by his grasp of the complex proceedings.

He shrugged. "Probably something stupid. The prince has pointed out that there's danger in sharing the secret. It could be used against Granadure as easily as it's used against Obrion."

"If they ever tried that, the king would send the

tertiaries against them. Weakening agent won't help them when they're overwhelmed by fire and water and earth."

Erich nodded but said, "Except Obrion might decide it's the perfect time to invade while we're distracted."

That was a disturbing point that she worried about as she continued her rounds. Half an hour later, while almost everyone was down in the formal gardens, enjoying a musical performance by an eighty-four-member orchestra, she received a summons to the prince's quarters on the third floor of the palace.

A little nervous, she was ushered right inside to a plush sitting room, carpeted with thick rugs. Prince Theodor sat in an overstuffed chair next to a couch where Captain Ilse and her husband, Commander Lukas, sat. Another couch and several more chairs, upholstered in floral patterns, were arranged nearby, around an ornate fireplace fashioned of delicate, green marble. Erich sat stiffly in one of the chairs. Across the room, a wide window showed a panoramic view of the formal gardens.

Prince Theodor rose from his seat to welcome her. "Welcome, Anika. Come in. I've heard good things about your work."

"Thank you, Your Highness," she stammered, making a battle maiden salute out of pure habit.

He gestured her to take a seat nearby, then resumed his own. "So organizing the florists into their first guild and recruiting them all to decorate Reizend better than it has ever looked before wasn't enough? I hear you also found the note and alerted security forces of the presence of a potential assassin. Good work."

"Thank you," she said again, hating how her face flushed under the prince's praise. He seemed relaxed and confident, gracious and kind. She felt completely unsettled in his presence. She usually knew how to react, and when she didn't she resorted to bluster and throwing down challenges to wrestle. She couldn't do any of that with the prince.

The very thought of challenging Prince Theodor to wrestle made her face feel hot. She wished she could hide for a few minutes to compose herself.

Prince Theodor thankfully turned away. Anika glanced at Erich, who was silently laughing at her.

The prince said in a more businesslike tone. "Now that we're all here, let's get to it. We don't have much time, but I felt it important to meet. Intrigue is common at such events, but the discussion of poison is a serious breach of etiquette. Worse, I don't like the idea of a secret Petralist in my home, particularly one skilled enough to slip past my guards and your watching Longseer to retrieve that note. Are there any new leads?"

"Nothing yet," Lukas said. He was muscular and carried himself exactly as the commander of a special-forces unit should. His most prominent feature on his weathered face was a huge, bristly mustache.

"Then we must dangle a prize before them that they cannot ignore."

Lukas said, "I do not recommend you expose yourself to any danger, Your Highness."

Prince Theodor chuckled. "I may be a target, but during this summit, I'm not the prize."

"You mean the weakening agent," Anika guessed.

He nodded. "Exactly. The entire summit is revolving around the question of the powder."

Anika stifled a sharp intake of breath. She hadn't even known the agent was a powder, but it made sense. If powdered granite could trigger superhuman strength, why not some other powder to counter it?

The prince continued. "I don't know how knowledge of its

existence spread so wide so quickly, but I suppose I shouldn't be surprised. The more dangerous the secret, the less effectively it can be kept. The Arishat delegates are desperate to get their hands on it, and I cannot imagine that Obrion has not also heard about its existence. They would have to move against it, and this summit offers the perfect opportunity to do so."

"We have no concrete proof that Obrioner agents have infiltrated your palace," Lukas said.

The prince met his gaze and asked, "Can you honestly say you don't think they're here?"

He hesitated, and Ilse poked him in the side. "Just say it, Lukas. Your hesitation already has."

He sighed. "They are probably here."

Prince Theodor said, "That fact does not reflect poorly on you or your company, Commander. You're a recent addition to my security team, and this summit has been in the works for months. Enemy agents have had plenty of time to prepare their strategy."

"Will you cancel the summit, then?" Erich asked.

The prince chuckled, "And waste this opportunity? No, my powerful friend. We have the chance to capture an extremely skilled Obrioner spy, one who has infiltrated my palace, despite all our efforts to prevent it. We must catch them."

"And perhaps even snare the Arishat League in a compromising position," Ilse suggested.

Prince Theodor grinned. "Even better. I could leverage that for tremendous advantage in our negotiations."

Anika listened carefully. She felt immensely proud that she'd deduced some of the same ideas they were discussing. She'd expected the prince to be furious that his palace had been infiltrated, and approved of the fact that he instead focused on the advantages the situation presented.

Ilse said, "So you plan to use the powder to draw them in, yes?"

The prince grinned. "Indeed, I do."

"You have some here in the palace?" Lukas asked.

When the prince nodded, Erich frowned, and Anika felt her own shiver of unease. What would it feel like to suffer the effects of such a powder? She tapped a bit of her granite strength and savored the power that flowed across her torso and down her limbs. As always, the feel of it bolstered her confidence.

Prince Theodor said, "I suggest a demonstration."

"You mean to test it on one of your own people?" Ilse asked, her expression unreadable.

"Unless you can provide an Obrioner to test it on." The prince glanced from her to Erich, who couldn't hide his frown. "I know the thought of testing this new weapon on one of our own is disturbing, but unless new clues are discovered before lunchtime tomorrow, I don't see any better choice. Besides, the effects are only temporary."

"You've seen the tests?" Lukas asked eagerly.

"More than seen. I've tested the powder on myself."

"Do you think that was wise?" Ilse asked. It was clear what she thought of the stupid idea.

"I needed to know personally what it can do."

Anika respected that, but agreed with Captain Ilse. Crown Prince Theodor was too important to risk in such a foolish way.

"You won't test it on yourself again here, though," Lukas said. It wasn't a question.

"Probably not. The effects are temporary, but very debilitating. I am afraid I must operate at full capacity to avoid falling for one of the Arishat's many devious contracts."

Lukas looked relieved. Ilse said, "Then you need a volunteer."

Anika tensed. It should be her. She was a Rumbler battle maiden, but during the summit she was just a florist. If she was temporarily debilitated, it wouldn't put anyone else at risk.

She took a deep breath, preparing to voice her thoughts.

"I'll do it," Erich said.

Anika stared at her brother, shocked beyond words. Erich looked calm, resolute.

The others looked just as startled. Ilse asked, "Are you sure?"

He nodded. "It should be me. I'm not one of the regular guards. There are plenty to cover for me while I'm down."

Anika finally found her voice. "No. It should be me."

Erich shook his head. "Your guild might need you. They might find another note."

"But . . . " She wasn't sure what to say. She'd never imagined her brother might possess such nobility, such willingness to sacrifice.

"I like it," Prince Theodor said decisively. "Thank you for offering, Erich. You'll make a perfect subject for the demonstration. Who better than our nation's champion Rumbler? If the powder can weaken you, it would weaken anyone else."

Anika wanted to protest, but Erich met her gaze and ever-so-slightly shook his head. He knew what she wanted to say, what she should say. Why would he tell her not to? She trusted him, but hated the thought of him suffering.

She hesitated, and the conversation moved on. They agreed to hold the demonstration the following evening, just prior to the formal ball.

Prince Theodor rubbed his hands together eagerly. "We'll hold the demonstration in the ballroom. I'll promise a second demonstration for the following morning in the music room, and we'll secure more powder in a locked cabinet there until morning."

Lukas guessed, "But that additional powder won't really be authentic."

Ilse grinned. "The spy won't be able to resist an attempt to get it, especially if we post a heavy guard around the room."

"Indeed," the prince said. "If they can sneak a note without alerting a watchful Longseer, why not infiltrate a guarded room?"

"Won't they know it's a trap?" Anika asked.

"They may suspect it, but they still can't possibly resist making the attempt," Lukas assured her.

Prince Theodor rose. "I must return to the summit before I am missed. I leave you to see to the arrangements."

After he left, Anika turned to Erich, who looked a little sick. "Why did you volunteer? You had to know I was going to."

"That's why I had to. There's no way I'm letting anyone test something like that on you before I try it out first."

Anika scowled to conceal her desire to hug him. She would not show weakness in front of Ilse. "I'm not a child, Erich."

"But you're still my little sister."

## 13

# NO ONE NEEDS TO KNOW WE'RE MAKING THIS UP AS WE GO

The next morning passed far too quickly. Anika covered miles of beautiful rooms and hallways as she moved between the stations of all the various girls, making sure they stayed focused. She double-checked every single floral arrangement for any sign of other clues. Her girls sensed her mood and focused on their work.

At least that's what she told herself. The fact that the delegates again remained closeted away all morning helped. The bulk of their entourages were not involved in the actual talks. The day dawned warm and pleasant, so most of them spent the morning walking the formal gardens, meeting in quiet conversations, and watching a series of theatrical performances down by the pond. That meant fewer handsome, tempting officials to distract her girls.

Anika chewed on the idea of going to Captain Ilse and insisting she be the one they test the agent on. She could not quite make herself do it, though. She didn't want to cheapen Erich's noble sacrifice or second-guess her captain and the prince himself. That didn't make it any easier for her to think about her brother falling to the devilish weakening agent.

She was summoned to meet briefly in Ilse's tiny office just before lunch to confirm no one had come up with any new leads. Lukas and Erich joined them a moment later.

"That's it, then. The prince plans to announce the demonstration during the luncheon feast. Are you ready?" Captain Ilse asked Erich.

He nodded, his expression determined.

Anika couldn't resist trying one more time. "Let me do the test."

Ilse shook her head, and Erich said, "You know you can't. The prince is going to announce me. Besides, having a secret Petralist concealed right in front of them all is perfect cover."

Ilse added, a note of reprimand in her voice. "We've gone over all of this already. I appreciate your concern for your brother, but orders are orders. If the prince himself has tested the agent and proved that the effects are only temporary, Erich can do no less than his duty."

Anika slumped, wishing she could say something more. Erich placed a hand on her shoulder and gave it a little squeeze. "We have plenty of backup in case something goes wrong while I'm still affected, and you'll be there to back up the rest of them."

Anika managed a little smile. Most days she yearned for a chance to punch Erich senseless. She'd never quite managed that. The thought of some unknown agent rendering her mighty brother helpless seemed insulting. She swore that she would protect him if the enemy attacked.

Anticipation grew to a feverish pitch as the afternoon wore on. Anika heard many excited conversations about that evening's demonstration. Some people did not seem to quite believe anything could render the mighty Erich help-less, and some even suggested the entire demonstration was a farce, a fabrication to gain leverage over the Arishat League. Others seemed far more ready to believe the agent was real, focusing on the potential critical advantage it might offer against Obrioner aggression.

Anika thought much about that too. Despite the potential risk that it could be used against Grandurian troops, it did offer a seemingly miraculous answer to the threat posed by Obrion. Granadure enjoyed many Petralists, but in a full war, Obrion would likely hold the advantage.

Their disgusting breeding program over the past three centuries had produced a growing number of powerful Petralists, many of whom were strong enough to unlock the coveted secondary and tertiary affinities. But the heart and soul of any Obrioner army was their Boulder bash fighters. If this new agent could really remove their strength, that single stroke could snuff out the core of any enemy assault.

Since it offered so much potential reward, Obrion and even the Arishat League would take unprecedented risks to get their hands on some.

Anika did not like worrying. It was not her nature. All her life, her Petralist power had been the rock upon which she built her confidence. Any threat, no matter the form it took, always seemed trivial compared to her granite strength.

Unfortunately, this problem presented no clear enemy for her to throw through a stone wall. She didn't like it. If these were the kinds of problems Captain Ilse faced regu-larly, no wonder Ilse was looking for more than average fighters. Usually Anika preferred getting pointed at an enemy and told to beat them to dust. Was she really ready to claim a position on Ilse's team?

With so many people there to witness the demonstration, the prince decided to hold it in Reizend's great hall. As soon as Anika heard that the meeting tables would be removed, she rounded up Sophie, Lulu, and a few other girls to make sure no one wrecked the beautiful centerpiece, and to ensure the hall was ready. They rushed along the east hall, barely slowing as they hurried through the grand entryway, passed under the suspended rain of flowers, and turned up the central hallway that led to the great hall.

When they arrived, they stopped in the doorway to stare. The long table had already been removed, and the huge centerpiece lay on the floor, its long wings, which had cascaded so beautifully down to the floor were severed.

Biberach was standing over it, a look of glee on his face. His voice echoed clearly across the great hall. "Just rip it apart. It serves no more purpose to us."

"No!" Sophie shouted before Anika could, and together they rushed into the room, with the other girls close on their heels.

Biberach greeted them with a smug look of satisfaction. "The prince gave orders to dismantle the table."

"Not like this," Sophie exclaimed, looking close to tears.

Anika wanted to punch Biberach's smug face over the formal gardens. The rest of his body could choose to follow, or not. She didn't care. With balled fists, barely resisting the urge to tap granite and smash him off his feet, she hissed, "I warned you not to touch our flowers."

Biberach retreated from her anger, his smug look fading to one of renewed fear. "But the prince gave orders."

"We came to take care of the decorations," Sophie said. "You had no right."

He stood taller and declared, "Lady Katrin herself assigned me to oversee the team removing the tables."

Anika said through gritted teeth. "Then take your tables and get out of here before I crush you into a ball of jelly."

Biberach was wise enough to scurry away. The workers who were removing the sections of the disassembled table exited through a side door, but Biberach headed for the main doorway. Sophie dropped to her knees beside the broken centerpiece, clearly fighting tears. Biberach looked back once and smiled.

Anika really wanted to go after him, but her girls needed her. She surveyed the damage. The arrangement had been broken into four large sections, like blue-and-white floral carpets. Each section looked fairly intact, but the overall effect had been destroyed.

Lulu touched Sophie's shoulder. "Flowers aren't meant to last long."

"I know," she said with a sigh. "But something this beautiful shouldn't be ripped apart with such carelessness, either." Sophie rose and met Anika's gaze. "I suppose we should drag all this out of the way before people arrive. I don't want anyone seeing it like this."

As the girls reached for the broken sections of flowers, Anika held up a hand. "Hold. We can do this a better way."

She refused to allow Biberach any victory, even one so small. He might have received orders, but he'd destroyed their work out of spite. They needed to salvage it, but how? It did need to be removed.

"I hear people coming," Lulu said nervously.

Anika glanced at the long, mostly-intact sections again and got an idea. She smiled. "We'll move them, but we'll do it with style."

"How?" Sophie asked, looking to Anika with desperate hope.

Anika hefted one section of beautiful, blue flowers, all woven tightly together. She flicked it into the air, like one might a sheet. As it spread out wide, she drew it over Lulu's head.

The girl froze in surprise, then giggled as the blanket of flowers draped over her like a soft, fragrant shroud. Anika pulled aside some of the flowers to create a hole for Lulu's head, allowing the blanket of flowers to settle to her shoulders like a gorgeous cloak.

"I like it," Sophie laughed, and she helped Anika place other sections over two of the other girls. Sophie wore the last.

Anika then hefted the long, shallow vase that held the beautiful, silver nebel flower and lebhaft roses. Holding it overhead, streamers of flowers draped down around her like a floral veil.

While the remaining girls checked on the other decorations around the perimeter of the room, Anika led the procession of flower-draped women out the great double doors. They emerged just as the first crowd of Arishat delegates and aides approached.

Instead of moving to the side of the hallway like she should, Anika held her course, walking at a slow, stately pace down the center. The foreigners stepped aside, grinning at the procession.

Lady Briet, the Althing delegate, stood near the front of the crowd. She bowed her head just a little, a smile on her lips. "I've never seen such a beautiful centerpiece. Nor have I witnessed a more fitting retirement procession. Well done."

"Thank you," Anika said.

Behind Lady Briet, one of her aides, a tall, handsome fellow, winked at Anika. She was so startled, she almost stopped. She felt herself flush, which made her annoyed. She was busy, trapped in the procession, unable to challenge the bold fellow to wrestle. She hated missed opportunities.

Sophie couldn't resist the urge to perform in front of a

crowd. Smiling brightly, she started to spin. The cloak of flowers flared around her dramatically, and her white dress with its bright, blue sash made an excellent counterpoint to the spinning, blue carpet of flowers. She added a graceful bobbing motion to enhance the effect.

The other girls followed her lead. They couldn't move with her dancer's grace, but they started to twirl to appreciative claps, and more than a few called invitations to meet later. Pretty young Lulu, her face flushed, grinned more happily than Anika had ever seen.

Anika hoped she didn't encourage the appreciative men too much. Maybe as part of the guild training they should include wrestling practice. She would not have her girls flirting without knowing how to defend their virtue in the face of determined admirers.

Twirling and dancing, the floral procession moved down the central hall, with all of those important people stepping out of their way. Anika let herself enjoy the moment, adding a few spins herself.

Then she spotted Biberach. The weaselly little many looked thunderstruck as he stared from their procession to the appreciative crowd. Anika caught his eye and shared a quick, victorious smile.

He glared, hatred in his eyes, and she realized he would never stop attacking their work until he found a way to undermine this victory.

Wonderful. She matched his glare before moving on. She'd have to find some time to speak with Sophie and discuss ways to break all of Biberach's fingers, and probably his teeth, in a way fitting Reizend's demands for high-society behavior.

Not until they passed through the crowds, twirled through the main entry hall, and proceeded down the east wing did they stop at a small storage room near Lady

Katrin's office. The girls were still smiling as they reluctantly folded the flowered cloaks into the storage room.

Sophie hugged Anika. "Thank you!"

"That was so much fun," Lulu agreed with a final happy spin.

"You all did great," Anika told them. "Come on."

She led the way back to the great hall. They'd retired their flowers with honor, but couldn't miss the presentation of the weakening agent.

During their brief absence, the enormous room had filled with several hundred eager spectators. If an assassin or spy tried to make trouble there, the many soldiers in attendance could swarm them under while the large exits would let civilians and noncombatants leave the area quickly.

Anika did not expect trouble during the presentation, but she had absorbed a little granite powder through her skin earlier, just in case.

The prince stepped into the center of the hall and raised his hands for quiet. The excited murmuring died quickly, replaced by soft shuffling as people shifted position to get the best possible view.

"My friends, it is my great pleasure to welcome you to this evening's demonstration. As you shall witness, this remarkable new breakthrough offers the potential to change the balance of power across the continent. Most of you know Erich, our national Rumbler champion. He has graciously offered to act as the subject of our demonstration."

He turned to his left and extended a hand. Erich strode out of the crowd to join him in the middle of the room. Erich looked massive and deadly in his Rumbler battle leathers. The shifting plates and many straps and buckles seemed to radiate danger. He wore a grim expression and did not bother waving to the enthusiastic applause.

The prince drew from a deep pocket inside of his jacket a small, ornately carved wooden box. All around the room, people leaned forward, eager for a peek at the treasure concealed in the box.

The prince gestured Erich closer and ten servants rushed forward carrying screens of dark blue cloth. They held them up like temporary walls around Erich and the prince.

"Lady Briet exclaimed, "What are you doing? We need to see how it is administered."

The other delegates called out similar complaints, and the murmur of angry muttering circled the room. Those already inclined to disbelieve the veracity of the demonstration loudly proclaimed the entire proceeding was a sham.

Then the temporary walls were whisked away, and the prince held up his hands for quiet. Erich looked no different. If anything, he looked angrier.

The prince proclaimed, "Today's demonstration is simply that. A demonstration. The full properties of this weakening agent, along with its manner of administration are still considered state secrets. We have not reached the stage in our negotiations yet for those secrets to be revealed. However, you came for a demonstration, and you'll get it."

He paced around Erich, who remained motionless. "You're all aware of Erich's reputation. He is an accomplished warrior, capable of beating most opponents without even drawing upon his granite strength. When he taps granite, no one, not even our most accomplished bash fighters, have stood against him. Tonight we shall demonstrate that under the effects of this weakening agent, Erich would fall to the weakest of foes."

The Varvakan general stepped forward, hand on his

sword. "Fine, I volunteer. Come fight me and prove you are weak."

That offer seemed to please most people in the room. A ripple of agreement spread from the boisterous Varvakan assembly to the other delegations. Anika suddenly feared for her brother's safety. The general was known as a mighty warrior. He could easily dispatch a weakened Erich and claim it was only an accident. No doubt his people would eagerly spread the word back in their home country that he had single-handedly defeated Granadure's mighty champion.

She couldn't let that happen. She took a step away from the crowd, but hesitated, not sure what she could do without making matters worse.

The prince smiled graciously and said, "I appreciate your offer, my friend. No one doubts your willingness to do battle against any foe, unfortunately that is the problem. If you were to defeat Erich, there may still be some lingering doubt about the effectiveness of this weakening agent. You are, after all, an accomplished warrior. No, we cannot leave any room for doubt. We shall have him face a noncombatant."

The prince turned slowly, scanning the room, as if considering who to nominate to face the huge Erich. People might have been loudly complaining that the demonstration was a sham, but those same people shrank under the prince's stare, clearly worried that he might invite them to put their doubts to a very real test.

The prince finished his circuit, facing Anika. He pointed directly at her. "And the perfect solution stands right there before you."

Anika wasn't sure what to do. He couldn't choose her. Sure, she had battled Erich more than anyone living, but she was a battle maiden even more than she was a florist. It didn't make sense.

As everyone in the room turned to look at her, the prince added, "Who better to prove the effectiveness of this demonstration than a simple florist?"

Anika gaped, not believing him. She was supposed to remain anonymous. Maybe he wanted to place her right next to her brother so she could protect him if something went wrong, but she wasn't a helpless florist.

The prince smiled warmly. "So I choose Sophie, the first-ever matron of the newly formed florist guild."

A gasp of surprise from behind Anika perfectly echoed her thoughts. Sophie stood there, cheeks flushing under the attention. But she recovered quickly and squared her shoulders. She stepped forward to stand beside Anika and raised a hand, her eyes bright, the picture of composure and beauty under pressure.

"If this was your idea, I'm going to make you snort a full measure of sneezing powder," Sophie hissed softly to Anika.

The closest spectators apparently took her brief hesitation as fear.

"Go on, dear. I'm sure it's perfectly safe," one richly dressed Althin urged Sophie. The woman was one of those who had been expressing doubt about the demonstration. She seemed ecstatic to watch someone else put the question to the test.

As encouraging cheering built around the room, Sophie moved with hesitant steps toward the prince. Anika stepped back into the crowd, feeling relieved.

Erich played his part perfectly. Amazing. Anika had never known he had any acting skills. He sneered and his deep voice carried easily across the room. "You've got to be kidding me."

"Don't worry, mighty warrior. I promise not to hurt

you," Sophie told him in a trembling voice. That triggered a round of laughter that sealed the agreement.

The prince gave Sophie an encouraging nod and stepped back several paces. He threw his arms out wide and said, "Let the contest begin."

Erich moved forward, and Sophie shifted to the left, looking decidedly nervous. She was clearly no warrior, but moved with a dancer's grace, her skirt swishing around her legs.

Anika watched in growing concern. She wasn't concerned for Sophie, but feared what was about to happen to her brother.

The Varvakans began to cheer Sophie on, urging her to throw a punch. Others soon took up the cry, and Erich looked disgusted by it.

He lunged, grabbing for her as if to lift her off the ground. His already impressive bulk swelled with granite, and the ominous creaking of his leather armor momentarily stilled the excited cries across the room.

Sophie shrieked and caught his hands. Just as she gripped him, her expression of fear changed to astonishment. Erich staggered, a look of surprise flashing across his face as his eyes rolled back and he collapsed with a groan. He lay in a crumpled heap at Sophie's feet, looking like he had simply died.

An astonished gasp rippled across the room, and Anika clenched her fists by her side, fighting the overwhelming urge to rush to her brother's side. Even though she'd known that would happen, seeing him lying helpless before so many filled her with terror and a fierce desire to protect him.

Sophie dropped to her knees beside Erich and reached out to shake him. He made no reaction, although as Anika watched closely, she noted his chest rising with a faint breath. He was alive, if only barely.

Relief swept through her, nearly dragging tears to her eyes, but she blinked them away quickly. The emotion was instantly replaced by seething anger. She looked toward the prince, standing in the center of the room near her fallen brother, and she was sorely tempted to march up to him and knock him to the ground to lie beside Erich.

Before she could, dozens of eager spectators rushed forward to see for themselves. Briet led the way, with of the Varvakan general half a step behind, followed by the other delegates and their aides.

They pushed and jostled for a chance to check on Erich, feel his weak pulse, and verify that he was not faking injury. Anika felt overwhelmed by fear for her brother and pushed through the crowd to get close to her brother and Sophie, who held her ground next to him. This would be a perfect time for someone to try to assassinate Erich.

Lady Briet exclaimed, "This is no sham. I saw him swell with granite, but there is no trace of strength in him. He seems completely comatose."

As her words were repeated over and over again through the crowd to those who were as yet unable to press in close to the fallen warrior, the Varvakan general extended a hand to Sophie and helped her rise. The crowd gave her a little room.

He general laughed. "Well done, girl. You stood your ground bravely. What is your name?"

Anika couldn't read what Sophie might be feeling. Sophie spoke clearly, showing no hint that the important people surrounding her intimidated her. "Sophie."

"A strong name for a strong and beautiful woman." He leaned a little closer and whispered something into her ear.

By her sudden flush and look of surprise, Anika guessed he'd made a bold invitation.

She drew closer behind the man, ready to throw him through the gilded ceiling if he didn't back off. Lucky for him, he moved away and the crowd pressed in around Sophie, sharing their congratulations. More than a few added soft, whispered words of their own, although Sophie's expression did not suggest what they said.

Anika could guess. It seemed the thought of spending time with the pretty girl had stood boldly before Erich seemed extremely alluring. Sophie weathered the storm with poise and grace. Anika stayed close to watch over her and Erich both.

The prince gave the crowds a full ten minutes to gawk before sending in Healers to tend to Erich. Under their administering hands, he coughed and moaned and tried to sit up, but fell back again. That elicited new exclamations of wonder. No one doubted any longer the potency of the weakening agent.

Prince Theodor spoke, his voice magnified by a Longseer. "This concludes tonight's demonstration. I have enough weakening agent for a second demonstration in the morning in the music room. That will give you time to consider what you've just seen."

"Can I see the weakening agent before you consume it all?" Lady Briet asked, not trying to conceal her eagerness.

"Not yet. If negotiations prove successful, then I will send for another sample to show to select individuals."

The delegates did not look happy about that, but everyone else seemed satisfied by the demonstration.

Anika silently hoped the prince was right about the trap. Erich's sacrifice had better not be for nothing. Any conspirators now had a deadline. If they failed to steal the weakening agent before the morning's demonstration, they'd lose their chance. Any spy worth the name would easily learn the location of the safe where the secret would be stored.

She hoped they would make an attempt. She really wanted to hit someone who deserved it.

## 14

## CLOSING THE TRAP

Reizend buzzed with excited chatter as the crowds dispersed. Prince Theodor had not only secured a powerful negotiating position, but he'd stirred up everyone into a frenzy. Anika heard dozens of ideas about the nature of the weakening agent, how it was administered, how it worked, and how long the effects might last. Even if the spy was reluctant to move against the weapon, they could no longer hesitate. They needed to get their hands on that agent, or someone else would.

When it was clear Erich was not in immediate danger, Anika slipped away, intending to ask Prince Theodor how soon he might recover. Unfortunately, the prince was surrounded by a knot of aides and officials.

Chief among them were Lords Leuthold and Ramwold. Anika had seen them only a handful of times, and they always seemed to be arguing. At the moment, the argument revolved around the presentation.

Anika drew closer and studied them. They were among the most important lords at the summit. If the prince was not the target of the poisoning, might one of them be instead?

Lord Ramwold was a heavyset man, his muscular youth fading to flabbier elder years. His silver hair and lined face suggested that although not exactly old, he was far from young. He was speaking loudly and with a noted lack of respect to Prince Theodor, stamping a silver-tipped cane for emphasis.

"You can't be serious. A second demonstration is bad enough, but you all but promised to show them the agent. This cannot be tolerated."

The prince accepted his railing words without looking offended, and Lord Leuthold responded instead. "Think before you bark, my dear Ramwold. The second demonstration will consume the last of the agent we have here in Reizend. What better way to remove the temptation and the opportunity than to use it all up? That way the prince controls when and if any closer inspections are to be allowed."

Lord Leuthold was surprisingly young for one who held so much authority and the ear of the prince. He looked barely thirty, richly dressed, brown hair glistening with styling oils. His hazel eyes seemed to rove constantly. To Anika that suggested he lacked focus, but she'd also heard that he was a crafty businessman and adept politician. He had increased his family's holdings and political position significantly in the few short years since he'd inherited.

As Lord Ramwold opened his mouth to argue further, Prince Theodor raised a calming hand. "Rest easy, my friend. I will not lightly share any more with anyone. Cheer up. Tomorrow's negotiating session should be enjoyable, especially for you. I will look to you to take the lead and to leverage to full advantage the position we now enjoy."

That seemed to please Lord Ramwold immensely.

Lord Leuthold said, "And to celebrate tonight's success, I have a special bottle of wine, shipped all the way from Sehrazad, that I would like to share with you, my prince."

Prince Theodor chuckled. "I'd be happy to drink your wine for once, Leuthold." Then he headed for the main exit, trailed by his entourage. Anika followed, still hoping to catch his eye, but Lord Leuthold kept his attention.

"Your highness, I must inquire as to status of the documents I presented yesterday. Perhaps while we drink that wine--"

The prince waved away the question with a good-natured laugh. "Not now, Leuthold. We'll deal with that when we complete the summit. That mountain's not going anywhere."

"Of course," Lord Leuthold said smoothly.

The prince turned to speak with another aid. Anika turned away. It was obvious she wouldn't get the prince's ear any time soon and she needed some quiet time.

She headed out into the formal gardens. There, she paced the shadowed, complex maze as twilight crept across the land. She breathed deep the clean evergreen scents and the aromas of the many blooming flowers. Those smells helped center her mind. She needed to be ready for whatever dangers might present that evening.

She heard others moving about in the maze, but she avoided them. If she ran into any of those men who had made their bold invitations to Sophie, she doubted she'd be able to conceal their screams from other people.

Eventually she returned to the back patio, sprinkled lightly with guests. Most summit attendees had returned to the grand ballroom for the opening of the evening's ball. Men were dressed in their finest suits or parade uniforms, while the ladies dressed in elegant gowns, and many of them dripped with expensive precious stones.

Anika never understood why people would pay so much for a ruby or an emerald, but pay so little for an equally lovely flower. Even better, why not spend one's fortune for more power stone? Flowers would eventually wilt, and those bits of colored stone possessed no magic. Only granite, marble, or obsidian offered real benefits.

She stepped into the ballroom to catch a glimpse of the richly-dressed nobility as the band struck up the tune for one of the complex dances popular in such settings. She caught sight of the prince's wife, her highness, Lady Adelaide.

The beautiful, elegant woman instantly captivated the crowd as she swept through the ballroom to join her husband at the high table. She wore a gorgeous crimson and blue gown, her long, golden hair woven into intricate braids. She wore a tiara set with diamonds and rubies, with a piece of limestone positioned directly over her forehead.

Anika was not aware of Lady Adelaide's affinities, if any, but either she was a Solas, or she had asked one of her Petralists with that gift to touch the limestone. It admitted a soft light, just enough to draw the eye and reflect through the other glittering stones in her tiara. It surrounded her in a unique halo that confirmed to all who saw her that she was indeed royalty.

That kind of style Anika appreciated.

Most of the other florists were in attendance, dressed in their finest. They made a pretense of checking the flowers, but most watched, enthralled, and more than a few were invited to join the dancing.

Anika left before anyone attempted to ask her to dance. She didn't feel like celebrating yet. Instead, she made another round to check the decorations and those florists she hadn't spotted in the ballroom.

She already considered them her girls, and Anika hated

the thought that any of them might consider casual submission to a potential romance. Women not trained as battle maidens often did not understand the importance of wrestling. Most would rely on the honor duel challenge by a brother to defend their honor, but they should be willing to stand up for themselves.

Feeling a bit morose, she returned to the patio, enjoying the cooler night air. More and more guests were exiting the ballroom and moving in pairs or small groups along the stone-paved expanse. Anika circled them, moving to the deeper shadows below the overhanging balcony. Unfortunately, several couples moved in that direction, clearly planning to enjoy a more intimate moment in the deeper shadows than they could out in the light.

Anika doubted she would ever act so foolish. She certainly had never yet met a man she might consider eventually surrendering to. She was starting to wonder if she ever would.

Banishing those depressing thoughts, she moved out from under the balcony to give space to the amorous couples. She'd barely gone twenty feet when a deep groaning emanated from the wooden supports under the balcony.

Anika spun and looked up, as did the couples standing beneath the balcony. With a sharp crack, the center support snapped, followed in quick succession by several others. With a shrieking groan of splintering wood and bending metal, the entire balcony gave way.

Anika reacted on pure instinct, lunging forward and max-tapping granite. Strength roared through her, transforming her into a perfectly sculpted stone goddess.

She caught the falling balcony.

It was heavy, unbelievably heavy, but Anika threw herself into the challenge, unleashing every ounce of anger at what had happened to her brother, coupled with her frustration that they had not yet found the assassin. Shouting with the strain, she locked her muscles and dug deeper from granite than she ever had in her life.

She held it. For a dumbfounded heartbeat or two, the couples that had been screaming in terror as death plummeted toward them could only gape in astonishment as Anika stood over them, holding up the entire balcony. More partygoers, caught on top of the balcony when it collapsed, were piled along the railing in a tangle of limbs.

"By the Tallan's grace, get out of there!" she bellowed.

The couples trapped beneath scrambled out of the way, and the people on top disentangled themselves, slid off the end when she tipped it to the ground, and ran to safety. When they were all clear, she allowed the rest of the balcony to drop with a heavy thud onto the patio.

The din had drawn everyone's attention. Soldiers rushed in from every side, weapons held uselessly at the ready. Other guests approached, gasping in astonishment at the balcony and at Anika's unexpected strength.

That same handsome Althin who had winked at her when she led the floral dance procession recognized her. "Wow. You're beautiful and strong too. With your skin like that, you look like a living rose."

He smiled invitingly, and Anika groaned to herself. She released granite and faced him, hands on hips. He was from Althing, so lacked any affinity, but he was good looking.

So she winked and said, "In Granadure, when a man admires a woman, we wrestle."

"Sounds fun," he said, drawing a bit closer.

She smiled, approving of his bravery. Even a halfway-decent wrestling match would feel wonderful. "I've only broken thirteen bones of men who invited me to wrestle. Most broke their arms or wrists, but a couple had weak ankles." His smile faded so she added quickly. "The prince has excellent Healers."

The man's eager expression turned to a look of concern. "Uh, I think I hear my leader calling. Please excuse me."

"Maybe later, then," Anika said, even though it was clear there would be no later.

The man fled.

Anika was tempted to extract the pouch of sneezing powder she carried in a pocket and throw it at the coward. Let him sneeze his yellow guts across the manicured lawn. It would serve him right for daring to make advances on a girl without possessing the heart to defend his interest.

International diplomacy could be so disappointing.

At that moment, one of the huge, many-tiered fountains on the first tier of formal gardens exploded. Bits of stone erupted in every direction, some raining down among terrified guests or pinging off the walls of the palace. One large chunk smashed through a second story window with a crash.

The waters of the fountain erupted three hundred feet into the air in an enormous column that held its shape before suddenly spraying outward in every direction. The waters swept across the lawns, knocking guards and richly dressed civilians from their feet.

A dozen voices shouted the alarm in unison. "Water Moccasin!"

Or, more likely, in Obrioner Spitter. As guests scattered from the destruction sweeping toward the patio, guards rushed to meet the threat, shouting for the prince's Water Moccasins to join the fray.

Anika sprinted the other way, into the palace. She had no idea who had attacked the balcony or triggered the explosive fountain flood, but it didn't matter. She understood what it meant.

Those were distractions.

Chaos was spreading throughout the palace with word of the outdoor attacks. About time. She was eager to close with a real enemy, not bandy words with cowards. Anika burst into the ballroom and spotted Captain Ilse and Commander Lukas with guards surrounding the prince.

Prince Theodor looked remarkably calm, although his face was flushed. He was issuing orders to mobilize his guard, secure the palace, and protect the delegates.

As Anika rushed toward them, Captain Ilse said, "Your Highness, I think you should retire to your quarters until we determine the nature of the threat."

Anika expected the prince to brush off her suggestion, but instead he said, "Of course. Good idea."

Captain Ilse looked surprised, as did most of his aids. Lord Leuthold shouted, "You heard His Highness. Let's get him to his quarters. If I may, Your Highness, I will accompany you."

"Of course, my friend," Prince Theodor said immediately.

"And perhaps we should invite Commander Lukas to join us for security," Leuthold added.

"Good idea. Commander, join us, please."

"I'd be honored," Lukas said. He too looked a bit flushed, probably eager to leap into battle, but he accepted with remarkable grace his prince's command to leave the potential fight.

Captain Ilse recovered from her surprise quickly. "Go, then. Everyone else, remain here." As the prince left with Lord Leuthold and Lukas, followed by several additional guards, Ilse ordered the prince's remaining guards to secure the ballroom and gather everyone else there for safety.

Anika waited impatiently until Ilse turned and said simply, "Report."

"Captain, at least two different distraction assaults launched at the rear patio."

"Poison?"

"No. Collapsed balcony and elemental water out in the gardens."

Captain Ilse nodded, then grinned eagerly. "The assault on the weakening agent has begun. I've got a squad of Crushers concealed around the safe in the music room. Come on, or we'll miss the capture."

Together, they ran for the door.

## 15

## ONE SPY, TWO SPIES, I SPY, YOU SPY

Getting from the ballroom to the music room took a frustratingly long time. Crowds of nervous men and women blocked the doorways and packed the wide eastern wing hallway halfway to the music room. They pestered Captain Ilse with questions about what was going on. While she tried to reassure everyone that the situation would soon be resolved, Anika slipped past her and through the crowd.

No one cared to ask a simple florist any questions. She had never considered that her simple white dress might ever prove more useful than her favorite leather battle armor.

Anika pushed through the last vestiges of the crowd and accelerated into a run down the east wing. That section of the wide hallway was mostly empty, all the way past the music room where the safe with the fake weakening powder had been set up to trap the spy.

At that moment, a large company of soldiers poured out of the music room and marched into the hall, escorting a black-garbed stranger away from the ballroom and toward the grand entryway. Anika accelerated to catch them, annoyed that she'd been delayed so long. She had wanted to help subdue the spy.

No one looked injured, not even the spy. Had the man actually surrendered without a fight? What a waste. If that was the best mettle Obrion had to offer, maybe her country shouldn't worry so much about a potential war with their southern neighbors.

Anika spotted Erich at the back of the company, struggling to keep up. She rushed to catch up with him and tried to slip one of his arms over her shoulders.

He shrugged it off and snapped, "Stop it. I'm fine."

"Sure you are. If you collapse at my feet again, I'll try not to step on your face as I walk past."

He gave her a rueful grin. "Sorry. I shouldn't be cranky. We got him."

"You're not used to being as weak as other men. It's a good lesson in humility," she told him.

He gave her that annoyed big brother look, and she felt relieved. He'd be all right.

Anika looked forward to the spy and his heavy escort. "Seems too easy."

"Not as easy as it seems," Erich chuckled. "The man's clever. Slipped inside without anyone noticing. Cut a hole in the roof and slid down a rope."

"And no one heard?"

"Pathfinder. Skilled one. I discovered him." Erich spoke with obvious pride. He might be barely able to hobble along the perfectly flat floor, but he'd played an important role in the capture, at least. "He tried to run. Swarmed up that rope like someone was hauling him up, but our Flameweaver severed it. Didn't have a choice but to surrender after that."

Captain Ilse caught up with the company as they approached the grand entryway. Back the way they'd come, curious onlookers craned to see what was going on. The company stopped to allow Ilse to survey the prisoner.

When she heard he was a Pathfinder, she frowned and said, "Notify the patio contingent. His partner is still at large."

"I work alone," the man said. He spoke in perfect Grandurian.

"Don't bother lying. Only a Spitter could have made that mess with the fountain. So there's got to be someone working with you."

The spy looked surprised, then actually broke into soft laughter. "Never thought I'd get duped to take the fall for some other spy's victory." He shook his head slowly, a rueful grin tugging at the corner of his mouth.

Anika exchanged a glance with Erich and the two of them turned back toward the music room. They said at the same time, "There's another thief!"

Erich added, "Obrion committed *two* tertiaries to this mission." That was a tremendous risk and confirmed how desperately they wanted to steal the weakening agent.

Ilse reached the same conclusion just as fast. As Anika tried helping her brother back toward the safe, Ilse started shouting orders.

"You four, take the prisoner to the dungeon. Everyone else, back to the music room! We've got another thief to catch."

Most of the Crushers charged past, and Anika was sorely tempted to leave Erich to hobble after while she joined them. Seeing that body of eager soldiers racing toward another fight filled her with battle lust, and she quivered with the need to tap granite and resume her role as battle maiden.

But for that night, she was a florist, and her place was

with her brother. She glanced at Erich, wondering if he'd mind getting carried for a while.

He raised a warning eyebrow. "Don't you dare throw me over your shoulder."

"We could get there faster," she offered.

"No." Ilse slowed next to them. "We don't know when the second spy will strike, or if there's only one more. There may be others. Anika, you can move about without drawing suspicion. I need you to double-check the rest of the palace for anything else amiss. Erich, return to the ballroom and assume command. Keep all the guests there."

Anika and her brother both saluted together, and she felt proud that she concealed her disappointment. She wasn't part of Ilse's team yet, still had to serve in her florist role.

And she loved that role. In it, she'd contributed critical intelligence. Ilse was right. Maybe she'd find the spy first. They wouldn't see her as a danger. She'd love to corral a dangerous Spitter alone. That victory would serve as a centerpiece to her service at the palace.

With a renewed sense of purpose, she told Erich, "Good luck".

He grinned and slowly followed Ilse, heading toward the distant ballroom. Anika turned her back on the Crushers and instead followed the squad of soldiers escorting the prisoner toward the entry hall.

It was time to hunt.

16

# IF ONLY SECRETS WERE FLOWERS, UNRAVELING THEM WOULD BE SO MUCH MORE FUN

The soldiers with their prisoner crossed the grand entry hall and continued down the western wing, but Anika turned toward the central hallway and the distant great hall. Alone, she paused in the beautiful entry hall and stared up at the rain of suspended flowers. It still looked spectacular, and she slowly breathed in the pleasant aroma of all those exotic flowers.

A loud crash of smashing pottery snapped her head around. She gasped at the sight of the elegant vase holding the Althing bouquet smashed, fragments of pottery and crushed flowers spread like a stain across the otherwise spotless floor.

Biberach!

The hated little man was fleeing toward the central hallway, laughing in delight at his destruction. White-hot fury erupted through Anika and she gave chase with a battle cry.

Biberach glanced back, but he was too full of hatred to even admit he'd made a fatal mistake. He met her gaze, flipped an obscene gesture at her, and taunted, "Do try to be more careful with your decorations, florist."

"Try winning the post of interior decorator with crushed hands!" she shouted back, tapping just a bit of granite to lengthen her stride. If she tapped too much, it would make her strides lumbering without really speeding her up a lot. A little granite strengthened her, but left her legs flexible and allowed her to move faster.

She grinned as she closed on the annoying little man. He finally started looking afraid as he tried to accelerate, glancing back nervously at her every few strides. That lack of focus only slowed him. She'd catch him before he reached the great hall.

Good. It was probably considered bad form to smear a cretin like Biberach all over those fancy walls. She hated that she hadn't yet discussed the best strategy for crushing him with Sophie. She wasn't sure of the right etiquette to follow.

He never reached the great hall. Halfway there, he abruptly turned and plunged through a concealed servant's door.

Annoyed that he was wasting even more of her time, Anika didn't even bother to check if he had locked the door behind her. She simply tapped more granite, applied it to her fist, and smashed the door off its hinges. She leaped through the splintered mess, barely twenty feet behind Biberach.

The echoes of the shattering door boomed down the narrow, plain corridor, and Biberach jumped. He glanced back again, but instead of begging for mercy like he'd done in the past, he stuck out a tongue at her and sprinted away.

Well, he tried sprinting. The scrawny waste of breath clearly wasn't used to running much. He was already gasping, but still staggered along with exceptional determination. She might applaud his tenacity in any other situation, but she was feeling too annoyed to applaud anything but her chance to finally wreak long-awaited vengeance upon him.

The narrow corridor emptied into a wide, windowless room, full of counters, shelves, and rolling carts. It looked like one of the many staging points for food and supplies before delivery to the great hall or other rooms in the palace.

And it wasn't empty.

A slender woman with jet-black hair, wearing a form-fitting leather jacket and leather breeches, stood in the room. A leather mask concealed her features, and she stood in the center of a free-standing whirlpool. Water rose around her in a swirling cone that reached up past her waist.

The enemy Spitter!

Anika skidded to a halt as the spy turned to face them. Biberach approached her, his expression victorious.

"What are you doing here, fool?" the woman snapped in heavily accented Grandurian. Her accent reminded Anika of the Sehrazad delegation, but Anika hadn't noticed anyone who looked remotely like her among them.

"I've brought the information you wanted," Biberach declared eagerly. He turned and pointed at Anika. "But I need you to dispose of this stupid florist for me."

Anika gaped. Biberach was working for the enemy? She'd known he was a small-minded, jealous, lack-talented buffoon, but she hadn't expected he possessed enough courage to betray his country.

Her anger at him solidified into a resolute determination to rip the man's head off. Heiderkraut take etiquette. She took an angry step forward.

The spy made no gesture, but water suddenly erupted off the floor and seized her in bands as strong as iron. Anika had not even noticed the thin sheen of water on the floor.

She almost tapped granite, but resisted the urge. To the spy, she looked like a florist. Her strength was her secret weapon. Her only chance against a Spitter was to lure her close enough to crush her skull in one overwhelming surprise attack.

Biberach laughed again, but the Spitter snarled, "Fool! I'm not here to do your bidding or settle your lover's quarrels."

"As if I'd ever consider him a worthy suitor," Anika said, disgusted by the idea.

Biberach looked equal parts shock, shame, and affronted pride. The effect twisted his unremarkable features into a hilariously contorted mask. "Now see here," he started, raising an angry finger.

Water sprang from the whirlpool and slapped him across the face, hard enough to leave a mark that looked like a woman's hand. That was a nice touch.

"Silence, fool," the woman hissed. "I gave you one simple task." She shook a little pouch at her belt, jingling coins within. "With the promise of more reward than you deserve. Nothing more."

"I have the information," Biberach cried quickly, raising placating hands. "The prince has retired to his chambers, and the Crushers are waiting to trap you in the music room."

"Traitor!" Anika shouted, struggling uselessly against her watery bonds. The temptation to tap her strength and lunge at him was nearly overwhelming, but she reminded herself she needed to think past the simple pleasure of crushing his skull. The spy was more important. Biberach would get his reward soon enough.

"You're a woman with some spirit, at least," the spy told Anika, her tone approving. "Why were you chasing this fool, anyway?"

"He broke one of my decorations," Anika said angrily.

The woman laughed. "Such small lives, filled with such insignificant concerns. You northerners are so useless."

"Let me out of these bonds, and I'll weave a wreath of iron roses around your face," Anika retorted.

The spy laughed again. When Biberach tried to protest, another whip-thin tendril of water lashed out and slapped him across the other cheek. He stumbled back, holding his face, looking affronted and afraid.

"Who are you?" Anika demanded. If the spy was willing to talk, could she distract her long enough for Ilse to realize the trap would never snare this woman? Would someone find the splintered door and send for reinforcements?

"You may call me Nuzha," the spy said, her voice cold.

"Why would you tell her your name, and not me?" Biberach demanded, his voice high-pitched and angry.

"Because I had planned to allow you to live to serve me another day," Nuzha replied in a deadly, cold voice.

"Wait!" Anika cried, but the conversation had apparently run its course. Nuzha made a negligent flick of her hand, and the waters of her whirlpool erupted across the room, the leading edge hardening like a thousand daggers.

The deadly tide swept Biberach off his feet in a bloody wave that churned across the room toward Anika. Nuzha saluted and turned away.

Anika tapped granite, just enough to harden her skin, but not enough to shift her form to sculpted lines. She hoped Nuzha didn't notice the tiny change.

The deadly wave crashed into Anika, swept her off her feet, and smashed her against the nearest wall. Spikes of water speared through her dress in a score of places, and the impact with the shelves on the wall drove the last of the air out of her lungs, despite the protection of granite. She fell in a heap among the shattered debris, and forced herself to lie motionless. If she got lucky, Nuzha would approach to check on her and she might get in a single punch.

No such luck. Nuzha left via a door heading deeper into the west wing. The waters boiled back across the room in her wake, leaving Anika, Biberach, and the broken shelves dry.

As soon as the door closed behind the spy, Anika heaved herself to her knees and crawled to Biberach. He lay in a crumpled pile nearby, his hair awry, one arm clearly broken, a deep, crimson bloodstain spreading beneath him.

Anika turned him over, and Biberach gasped, coughed water and blood, then grimaced, looking like he wanted to scream, but didn't quite dare. He'd been impaled in many places, his tattered shirt a mass of blood. Without a Healer's assistance, he wouldn't live long.

Anika needed him to survive for a bit, though. She leaned over him and touched his face. "Biberach? Can you hear me?"

He blinked a couple of times and focused on her. She was sorely tempted to punch him a couple of times, but that might just kill him, and she needed information first.

"She betrayed me," Biberach whispered.

Anika grunted. What a fool. "You betrayed your country. What do you expect?"

"No." Biberach shook his head weakly, tears dripping down his face. "Would never betray. Just wanted respect."

"You were used," Anika told him, surprised to feel pity for the poor, small-minded fool. "Why did she want that information?"

Biberach moaned and tried to shake his head, but failed. His eyes were glazing. He was succumbing to shock and would soon be of no use to her.

Anika slapped him. Gently. Well, almost gently. The

blow still snapped his head to the side and he cried out, then coughed again, then groaned.

That shook off some of his stupor and he glared at her. "Heartless."

"Stop whining. Your actions have placed the safety of our nation at risk."

"Didn't mean to," he whispered. He looked broken, his spirit crushed, his lifeblood draining away.

She'd heard many people felt a need to speak the truth at the end. Neither of them had time for any more stupid lies.

"What did you do?" she demanded.

"I set up . . . note between . . . Nuzha and Lord Leuthold. He promised--"

"Lord Leuthold?" Anika interrupted. That was a surprise. "What does he have to do with anything? Is he the one planning to poison someone?"

"Said no one . . . die," Biberach explained softly, his head lolling a bit to the side.

Anika resisted the urge to shake him. Instead she gently cushioned his head in her lap and asked, "Why use poison, then?"

"Help . . . deal. Promised me a promotion. I just . . . note. And today . . . wine."

"Wine?" Anika frowned, thinking back to Lord Leuthold's offer to share a special bottle of wine with the prince. Had they consumed it already? Was he planning to poison the prince?

Gripped by that new fear, she demanded, "Tell me quickly. What does the poison do?"

"Don't know. I swear by . . . Tallan's honor."

Anika glared. Intoning the Tallan's honor wouldn't help restore his own, but the information he was sharing might help. "Your treachery threatens the prince himself, you fool."

"No." Biberach blinked stupidly at her.

She ignored him, playing through her mind the memory of the last time she saw the prince. He'd looked flushed, had acted unusually compliant.

Could a poison do that?

Why hadn't anyone noticed that, inquired further? Because Leuthold had waited for the distractions that Nuzha and the Obrioner spy caused. Were they working together, or just leveraging each other's evil plots for their own gain?

She had to assume Lord Leuthold had poisoned the prince, who was now secured in his rooms with the very betrayer. Anika lowered the dying Biberach to the ground and leaped to her feet, terrified by thoughts of what Lord Leuthold might be planning.

"Don't leave me," Biberach begged.

"I'll send someone to help. If you live long enough, maybe you can face justice with honor."

A new fear chilled her. Lord Leuthold had arranged for Commander Lukas to join him and the prince. Lukas too had looked unusually flushed, had meekly accepted the unusual invitation.

"Thorns and blossoms!" Anika cursed, turning to sprint toward the main staircase. Behind her, Biberach cried out, his words indistinguishable, his tone pleading.

She didn't have time to comfort traitors. She wanted to return to Erich, explain what she'd learned, and send for reinforcements, but she lacked time. Ilse and most of the Crushers were distracted hunting Nuzha, and Nuzha knew it. Whatever she'd been waiting for, it seemed she was ready to strike.

And she hadn't been heading for the music room, but in the opposite direction.

Nuzha had duped them all. Their trap had been flipped back on them. Everyone was out of position, and a traitor in their midst might have arranged to deliver the prince into the hands of an assassin.

Anika ran faster.

17

## SOMETIMES THE TRUTH HURTS. SOMETIMES YOU JUST HAVE TO THINK WITH YOUR STOMACH.

As Anika rushed up the gently curving stairs to the third floor, she listened for fighting, but heard nothing. The palace was strangely quiet. The guests had been herded into the ballroom by the prince's guard, who were focused on securing them against enemy entry. Ilse and the Crushers were laying a trap that would never be spring.

Only Anika could reach the prince in time. So she ran, as the palace seemed to huddle in worried silence. She caught herself checking behind, worried Nuzha might leap out of hiding from anywhere.

The deadly foreigner could be anywhere, but Lord Leuthold was a known threat that she had to deal with first. If he had indeed poisoned the prince and Commander Lukas, what was his intent? Was he working with Nuzha? Did he intend to sell the weakening agent to her, or were their goals more nefarious? With the prince under his thrall, who knew what devilry he might engage in?

Who knew what crimes he might commit to cover his actions?

When she reached the secure western wing of the palace, it was blocked by a heavy oaken door, banded in steel. The blue paint, trimmed in gold vainly tried to depict the door as something other than a solid barrier. Four Rumblers stood at attention, barring passage.

Anika took that as a good sign. They would surely have reacted if they'd heard any kind of ruckus in the king's suite. Maybe she'd arrived in time, after all.

"What are you doing here, girl? And what happened to your dress?" the leader of the foursome asked when she approached, his voice concerned. He was a burly sergeant. They all looked competent and tough, but that wouldn't help if they'd allowed a secret enemy inside with the man they were trying to protect.

Anika glanced down at herself and grimaced. She looked terrible. Her dress was ripped, with several blood-stains from Biberach. She looked more like a casualty of war than a florist.

She couldn't do anything about that, so she pushed her hair out of her face and pretended everything was fine.

"Captain Ilse sent me. She's captured an enemy spy. I must report to Commander Lukas."

"I'm sorry, but you'll have to wait," the soldier said with honest-sounding regret.

"I can't. Captain Ilse ordered all haste."

"Captain Ilse doesn't override the prince. He gave strict orders not to be disturbed. He knows about the captured spy, and is personally interviewing him with the assistance of Lord Leuthold. Commander Lukas is acting as security."

"Quick, you have to get in there. The prince is in danger," Anika urged, stepping closer.

The sergeant raised a hand to bar her way. His companions watched with bored interest. A pretty florist in tattered clothing might help break the monotony of their watch, but they clearly didn't see her as a threat.

"It's time for you to leave, girl. Go get cleaned up. You're a mess."

"But--" she protested, stepping a little closer, trying to look exhausted and confused.

"The prince gave orders," the mana apologized.

She needed to get through, but her act wasn't working. So she changed tact. "The prince has been poisoned."

"How would you know that?" The man asked, sounding more amused than alarmed.

She opened her mouth to explain, but realized he'd never believe her. The story was crazy enough that she barely believed it herself.

That simplified things, but she felt bad for the men barring her way. They were only doing their duty the best they knew how. It wasn't their fault they were aiding and abetting a criminal.

But the truth was the truth, and sometimes the truth hurt.

So Anika max-tapped granite. Her skin hardened and changed hue while her body shifted to perfectly sculpted lines.

"I'll have to show you." She lunged.

The soldiers were experienced veterans. They reacted quickly. Two of them reached for swords, while the sergeant and his closest companion simply set themselves to meet her, their adjustable leather armor creaking ominously as their bodies swelled with granite strength.

They might be tough, but Anika had trained for months, battling her brother, the champion bash fighter of Granadure. Besides, she didn't need to beat them. She just needed to help them see the truth.

So Anika simply tucked her shoulder and plowed into

the sergeant. They collided with a loud crack of stone and leather, and she drove him off his feet. As the other soldiers moved to intercept, Anika gripped the sergeant's torso and plowed forward with all her strength.

The soldiers had expected a fight, not a pushing match so they were not set property. She might not be able to beat her brother in a direct contest of strength, but she never gave the men a chance to gain equal footing.

As a solid group, they slammed into the heavy door with grunts of breath blasted from their stone-enhanced lungs. The door groaned and creaked under the pressure, but by heiderkraut, it refused to burst. Anika kept her head tucked close to the sergeant she was using as a battering ram, trying to ignore his rock-hard fists that he beat uselessly on her back. His companions got caught in a hopeless tangle of superhuman arms and legs and torsos.

"You're dead, woman!" the sergeant bellowed, and grasped her hair, giving it a savage yank.

"You brute!" she shouted back.

A man in his position should know better than to grab at a girl's hair. She was trying to help them save their own prince, for Tallan's mercy! But a girl had to defend herself too.

So Anika slammed a fist between his legs, even as she kept up the pressure, driving the mass of soldiers against the door, which was beginning to groan under the pressure.

He might be tapping granite, but he still couldn't ignore a blow like that. He released her hair with a grunt.

Anika slammed into them again, shouting as battle lust swept through her and she max-tapped granite. Instead of her normal battle maiden war cry, she shouted, "Thorns and blossoms!"

It seemed appropriate.

And under that second assault, the door gave way, and

the five of them crashed through, sprawling together across the rich entry salon in a tangle of struggling limbs.

Anika tried to roll free, but the sergeant gained his feet first. Snarling, he grabbed her leg and yanked her off the floor. She swung upside down, lacking leverage to fight as he cocked back one arm to deliver a mighty blow.

But then his eyes slipped past her and he stopped, staring in surprise. Anika twisted in his grip and looked over her shoulder.

The Obrioner spy lay dead on the floor, a knife in his back, a pool of blood slowly spreading, seeping through the rich blue carpet.

The prince sat at an enormous desk, quill moving across a parchment in bold, fluid strokes. Lord Leuthold stood behind the prince, a dagger in hand. Commander Lukas sat calmly in a nearby chair, eyes closed. Was he sleeping?

"What's the meaning of this?" the sergeant demanded as his companions scrambled to their feet and spread out, facing Lord Leuthold. The lord looked frustrated, but said quickly, "Your Highness, order these men from the room."

"Leave us," Prince Theodor commanded.

No one moved.

"I told you," Anika said, tugging at her skirt, which was trying to slide up her legs as the sergeant held her in that unladylike position.

"Sorry." He flipped her around and sat her on her feet. She straightened her tattered dress the best she could and pointed at Lord Leuthold. "He's poisoned the prince with some kind of chemical that makes him obey."

Lord Leuthold looked shocked but said, "You heard your prince. Get out. My prince, please finish signing the document."

The prince smiled and obediently raised his quill again. The soft scratching of his writing seemed loud, and somehow punctuated the sense of impending violence that hung over the room.

"Why did you murder the Obrioner?" Anika demanded.

A quick scan of the rest of the office revealed no other threats. Thankfully she saw no sign of Nuzha. The office was huge, with enormous windows on the far wall that overlooked the formal gardens. To her right was a cold fireplace, with several comfortable chairs. A tiny, round table stood near the left corner of the desk, just big enough to hold a clear, glass vase of pale, yellow roses. Another smaller writing desk stood in the corner beside an oil lamp and a sturdy, simple chair.

She moved left around the soldiers, who stood facing the prince and Lord Leuthold. They all looked like they dearly wanted to swarm Leuthold, but didn't dare while he held that dagger.

"He's to blame for all this," Leuthold said. "Leave us, and we'll explain everything soon."

"You can't believe we'll leave now that we've seen your treachery," the sergeant said. "Drop the knife and perhaps the prince will spare your life when this is all over."

"Stay where you are." Lord Leuthold snatched up the parchment when the prince finished signing. His expression turned victorious.

The prince looked at them calmly and said, "Fetch someone to clean up that mess, will you?"

Anika marveled. What chemical could reduce one to such a state?

"That Obrioner attacked us and struck the prince with a strange chemical," Leuthold said quickly, his constantly roving eyes moving across them. "He did, didn't he, my prince?"

"All right," Prince Theodor said, looking bored.

"Step away from the prince," the sergeant commanded in a low, dangerous tone.

Lord Leuthold frowned and raised the dagger a fraction. "Back out of the room, or there will be more blood."

The soldiers clearly wouldn't retreat. Lord Leuthold looked desperate enough to do something truly rash. Commander Lukas snored softly from his chair.

Anika wasn't about to give Lord Leuthold time to commit another crime. She had no idea what that parchment meant, but it was clearly central to his plot. Might it be a royal pardon for his crimes? Would that even work?

He'd clearly committed treason and endangered the prince's life right in the middle of an international incident. If it was left up to her, his life would be forfeit.

"I am not in a patient mood," Lord Leuthold growled, sliding the dagger closer to the oblivious prince's throat.

The sergeant shouted, "Don't!" and the men tensed to charge.

None of them paid Anika any attention while she slipped off her shoe and threw it. She aimed for the dagger, but throwing a shoe wasn't quite the same as throwing a rock.

She hit Prince Theodor in the face and knocked him right over backward.

Oops.

Lord Leuthold hesitated for a second, looking startled. That was all the time the soldiers needed. They lunged across the room in a tide of stone-hardened muscle.

The sight of those men rushing him snapped Lord Leuthold out of his immobility. He raised the dagger and stepped toward the prince, who was struggling to sit up.

Anika swept the vase of yellow roses off the little table and threw it. This time her aim was true. She caught Lord Leuthold in the shoulder. The vase shattered and Lord

Leuthold tumbled away from the prince. The parchment slipped from his hand and drifted to the floor.

The sergeant reached Lord Leuthold half a second later, leaping right over the desk in a flying tackle and squashing the man back to the floor. The other soldiers threw the desk out of the way and rushed to help Prince Theodor to his feet.

Anika retrieved the parchment, which had rolled into a scroll. She pulled down the bottom where the prince's signature had smudged a bit from getting rolled up before completely dry.

"Careful with that!" Lord Leuthold shouted as the sergeant hauled him to his feet. His voice was a bit shaky, his hair messy, and blood on his face. He coughed after he spoke, wincing with pain. Hopefully he'd suffered several broken ribs.

"This is a lie," Anika said, waving the parchment at him.

"It's an officially signed document. It's legal and binding," Lord Leuthold said, struggling to maintain an air of dignity while the sergeant bound his arms behind his back. "Not even the prince himself can deny his signature now that it's affixed."

"But the prince is not himself," Anika protested.

"He'll recover shortly, and he'll have to verify the signature when he sees it."

Prince Theodor nodded, looking at his shattered desk with bemused confusion. He said, "Leuthold is right. Any authentic signature is valid."

"There's never been a case of a signature being made under duress?" she asked.

The prince shrugged. "I don't remember, but the legal proceedings could take years."

"Years in which I retain possession of lands with a

previously undiscovered power stone deposit," Leuthold chortled.

The soldiers looked disgusted, and Anika said, "Krokus! You betrayed your prince just to win a new quarry?"

It was reprehensible, but it wasn't the level of treason she'd feared. What connection did he have with the spy, Nuzha? Was he lying?

Lord Leuthold smiled, once again confident. "Florists shouldn't play with politics."

"True." Anika gave Lord Leuthold a charming smile. Then she ripped off the signature, crumpled the bit of parchment, and ate it.

## 18

## LOOK BEFORE YOU SNIFF

Lord Leuthold gaped, momentarily stunned. The sergeant laughed and clapped the lord on the shoulder, staggering him and eliciting a cry of pain.

The sergeant grinned at Anika. "Quick thinking, lass."

She returned the smile. The sergeant looked strong. He was decent looking, and he'd tackled Lord Leuthold with excellent style. She wondered if he liked to wrestle.

Before she could ask him, the plush office filled with a thunderous, rushing sound, and something struck her in the back, smashing her off her feet. If she hadn't still been tapping granite, the impact would have shattered her ribs.

The world spun around Anika, and she instinctively held her breath, even before she realized she'd been struck by water. That was important, but she couldn't think why with the water tumbling her around violently. She tried to struggle, but there was nothing to press against but the churning surf.

Panic swept through her and she lashed out helplessly in every direction. She couldn't see. The dark waters concealed everything, so all she saw were dark blurs churning around her. Her lungs convulsed, needing air.

That angered her. Dying so soon after saving the prince's life was worse than insulting. Again she lashed out, and she caught an arm. One of the soldiers. The man gripped her in return and she tried to pull him closer, but the churning water tore them apart.

Thorns and blossoms. She wanted to punch something, but she wanted to breathe more.

Then abruptly the spinning stopped. Her eyes cleared as dark water drained away from her face. She found herself standing in a column of water that held her firmly imprisoned, with only her head free. She struggled against the watery bonds, but despite her superhuman strength, she accomplished nothing. The water merely flexed around her, but did not relinquish its hold.

Anika glanced around. Everyone else was equally imprisoned, all lined up like prized bouquets on a shelf. Lord Leuthold looked dazed, but seemed to be breathing. Somehow Commander Lukas was still sleeping, his head lolling, soft snores blowing occasional bubbles. The prince was looking around with confused bewilderment, and the soldiers were all struggling mightily, but just as uselessly as Anika.

Movement in the doorway across the room drew her gaze. The black-clad spy stepped gracefully into the room. Nuzha studied them with a disapproving frown.

"You northerners are so disappointing. So busy fighting among yourselves, you left no guards outside." She made a tisking sound. "Bad form. You're not worthy of my daggers. The sooner I leave this cold, unpleasant country, the better."

"You'll never escape alive," the sergeant promised her with admirable, if laughable bluster.

Nuzha started to chuckle, but then she noticed Anika and her expression turned intrigued. She made a beckoning gesture, and Anika's watery prison slid forward a few feet.

"How by the blessed sands are you alive, girl?"

"I wasn't finished with you," Anika said coldly.

Nuzha chuckled and made a slow clapping motion, a mocking gesture. "Even more spirit than I'd thought. Perhaps not all northerners are stupid and soft."

"Release me and I'll show you how not-soft I am," Anika urged.

"Perhaps another day. I salute your spirit. May your knives ever remain sharp." Nuzha then approached Prince Theodor.

Anika tapped granite and strained against the watery bonds, as did the other soldiers. She could not bear to see the woman casually murder their lord.

The sergeant snarled, "Keep back, woman!"

A whip of water slapped him across the face. He ignored it. Hmm. He was indeed a fighter. Anika decided if they lived to see the next dawn, she would welcome an offer to wrestle with that man.

Nuzha sneered at the prince, who looked at her with a carefree expression. She said, "A ruler whose own subjects turn against him is weak, and needs not my dagger to prove it."

"Your accent is Sehrazad," Prince Theodor said in a conversational tone. "Few daughters of the sand travel so far north."

"And fewer still bandy words with northern barbarians," she snapped.

He took no offense, but nodded. "Indeed, you are renowned as women of action. What are you doing here?"

Anika tensed, afraid Nuzha would admit she planned to kill him.

She leaned closer and sniffed, then snorted in disgust. "Poisoned. No wonder. I wouldn't soil my blade with your flesh. No, fallen prince, I care nothing for your life. Deliver to me the weakening agent and I will allow you to live."

"Of course," Prince Theodor said. "It's--"

"Don't tell her," the sergeant interrupted.

Immediately, Prince Theodor snapped his mouth closed.

"Don't make me change my mind about leaving you alive," Nuzha snapped at the sergeant.

"I would gladly give my life to my prince."

"Even if it would accomplish nothing?" Nuzha sneered.

He clearly would, but that would be a waste of a good man. All Nuzha had to do was drown them and the prince would tell her the location of the powder. They had to resist, but couldn't they at least find a way to make that sacrifice mean something?

Suddenly Anika knew what she needed to do.

"I know where the weakening agent it!" she shouted.

"You?" Nuzha asked, glancing at her.

"Don't!" The sergeant shouted. Two more whips of water slapped him, then water flowed up over his mouth, sealing it shut.

"I'm sorry," Anika told him. "I cannot risk any harm to the prince."

"So tell me, girl with the heart of wisdom," Nuzha said.

"First you swear on your honor not to harm Prince Theodor."

"If you deliver the agent to me, I so swear," Nuzha said, placing her hand over her heart and making an odd gesture, with fingers closing together like the petals of a flower at sunset. "But if you fail to deliver it, I will rip out the heart blood of everyone in this room."

"You don't have to overdo the drama," Anika told her. "Too much gets old really fast."

Nuzha barked a laugh. "You have a valiant spirit. Now, I must depart. So give unto me the agent."

The waters flowed away from Anika, leaving her perfectly dry. She was grateful for that little courtesy. Her dress was tattered enough. If Nuzha had left it wet, it would have clung in a very immodest way. She didn't want to face such a deadly foe feeling embarrassed.

The sergeant struggled angrily in his prison. The other soldiers started shouting at her to stop, but Nuzha sealed their mouths without even looking at them. Lord Leuthold watched Anika with crafty interest, while the prince started humming a popular dance tune, his gaze drifting to the distant window. Lukas snored again.

Anika crossed to the smashed desk and reached into one of the drawers.

Nuzha laughed. "So much lack of imagination. You really keep such a valuable secret in your desk, prince?"

The prince chuckled, "Of course--"

"Stop, my prince!" Anika cried, interrupting. "She is beneath your dignity. Do not speak with her again."

Nuzha frowned from the prince to Anika. "I warned you, girl. Do not try my patience."

"I'm trying to avert a disaster," Anika assured her, rising from the desk. She hefted a tiny pouch in her hand. "Here's your agent. May you choke on it!"

She threw it with granite-enhanced strength. The little bag didn't fly as well as a rock, but over that short distance, the difference didn't matter.

Nuzha snatched for it, but the speed of the throw caught her by surprise, and the little bag of sneezing powder that Anika had drawn from her pocket while crouched over the desk smashed into the spy's face and exploded into a little cloud.

Nuzha gasped. "You fool! You've wasted--"

The rest of her words were lost as she sneezed so violently, her feet lifted right off the ground.

Anika max-tapped granite and lunged. Nuzha sneezed a second time, so hard she spat blood. She looked up, gasping, just as Anika pressed her finger to the center of her forehead and said, "Match."

Then she punched Nuzha in the jaw with her mightiest uppercut.

The look of shock on Nuzha's face as her head snapped back was priceless. The rest of her body followed. That punch should have ripped her head right off, but Nuzha's skin began shifting hue as she somersaulted right over the prince, smashed through the stone outer wall and tumbled away into the night.

"Heiderkraut!" Anika cursed. "She's a Boulder too."

The water holding everyone prisoner splashed to the floor and they staggered free. Anika gripped the sergeant's shoulder and met his gaze. "Get word to Captain Ilse. The enemy is outside."

Then she turned and leaped through the gap in the wall after Nuzha.

With any luck, Nuzha was dazed. Her granite affinity might have saved her life, but she might still be disoriented and vulnerable.

Cool night air rushed past, refreshing Anika and snapping her dress against her legs. She max-tapped granite and tucked her shoulder as she plummeted down toward the ground.

Anika struck like a living meteor, plowing three feet into the soft lawn. The brutal impact jarred her right through her granite-hardened body. She leaped up, shaking off dirt, and scanned for the enemy.

She'd landed behind the palace, near the formal gardens. A deep, furrowed trench nearby marked the spot where Nuzha had crashed to the ground, but she saw no sign of the woman.

"Thorns and blossoms," Anika growled. Behind her, an alarm bell began to sound. Good. Reinforcements would soon swarm the gardens.

Anika didn't plan to wait. She doubted Nuzha would return to the palace now. Most likely she'd fled into the formal gardens.

Anika raced into the darkness after her.

19

GOOD THINGS COME TO THOSE WHO
HOLD THEIR TONGUE. AND WRESTLE.

The next day, Anika approached the prince's quarters with Erich by her side. They wore their Rumbler battle leathers, her hair was braided, and a full measure of granite thrummed through her with the promise of superhuman strength. She felt nervous as she approached the same four guards stationed outside the battered looking entryway door.

She took comfort in the fact that Erich strode confidently by her side. The lingering weakness had evaporated overnight and he'd laughed like a little boy when he first tapped his power and his muscles swelled with undiminished strength.

As they approached the attentive guards, she met the gaze of the sergeant. She hadn't seen him since she'd leaped into the night after Nuzha. She felt satisfied with most of her performance the night before, but the failure of finding the cursed spy still frustrated her. The fact that Ilse hadn't been able to find her either, even with the help of her earth senses, helped her feel a little better.

The sergeant surprised her by snapping a smart salute. "Welcome, Battle Maiden Anika."

She returned the salute. Erich looked between them, surprised. Usually he was the one people saluted, but the guards barely seemed to notice him as the sergeant's companions all saluted along with him.

"Thank you, Sergeant. I hope you'll forgive my rash actions last time I was here."

He grinned. "On the contrary, you forced us to see the real danger. We owe you the honor of our station. Thank you."

He stepped forward and took her hand, bowing over it. Anika smiled, but hated the feeling of warmth rising in her cheeks. She would not blush in front of these men and ruin the moment.

The sergeant remained standing close when he completed the bow and added, "My name is Franz, and I would be honored to buy you dinner whenever you are free."

"I appreciate the offer," she said, giving him a dazzling smile. Yes, dinner would be nice, especially if it led to an epic wrestling match.

"I don't," Erich growled, reminding them both of his hulking presence.

Sergeant Fritz quickly stepped back into position, but did not look nervous at the prospect of Erich's wrath. Erich was eager to perform his brotherly duty to honor-duel any potential suitor. Maybe he'd finally get his chance.

"How do you like wrestling?" she asked Franz.

Erich scowled, but Franz grinned and said, "I've never lost."

Anika smiled. Better and better. "Neither have I." She was really looking forward to finding out if he was as strong as he seemed to think.

Erich's glare could wilt flowers, but Franz didn't seem to notice as he and his companions stepped aside and pushed open the door for them to enter. Erich marched past, scowling, and Anika followed with a final glance at Franz, who met her gaze but didn't bother trying any foolishness like winking. She thoroughly approved.

Prince Theodor's entry salon was already refurbished. The bloodstained floor was covered by a thick rug bearing the pattern of rolling Grandurian hills, the smashed desk and other furniture replaced by identical pieces.

An aide ushered them into a plush sitting room that Anika hadn't noticed the last time she was briefly in the apartment. Several overstuffed chairs were situated around a cheery fire that burned in a fireplace shaped like a gaping lion's mouth.

Captain Ilse and Commander Lukas sat on a nearby couch facing Prince Theodor. He also looked fully recovered, except for the shoe-sized bruise on his face.

Anika cringed to see it. Surely the Healers could have fixed that. The fact that they hadn't meant he'd ordered them to leave it. Did he plan to use it as a reminder of her folly, the justification for punishment? She'd only wanted to save him. She couldn't help it that the battle maidens never practiced shoe throwing.

She and Erich both saluted, and Prince Theodor returned the gesture. He smiled and motioned them to take seats to either side of Ilse and Lukas. "Welcome, and thank you for coming so quickly."

As if they could do anything but jump to obey the prince's command. Anika said, "It's our pleasure to serve in any way we can, Your Highness."

Prince Theodor chuckled and touched his face. "I don't doubt that for a second."

"I must apologize--" she began immediately, feeling herself flush with embarrassment.

He waved her to silence with a laugh. "Relax, my dear Anika. You have nothing to apologize for."

"I didn't mean to strike you. Really," she insisted.

"I believe you. You prevented a great deal of trouble with your bold actions, not the least of which was consumption of what could have been a very problematic document."

Erich chuckled. "She always did enjoy eating strange things."

"Surely you could have voided the document once you realized you were coerced," Anika said.

"The legalities are complex. I remember last night like a fuzzy dream, but I believe we did discuss that part."

She nodded and he continued. "No one ever likes to admit that a member of the royal house might not be competent to act. To nullify the document, I would have to publicly declare I was unfit. That could have opened the door to any number of complications. Since you consumed the signature portion of the document, proof of the transaction fell to Lord Leuthold, but he agreed to drop his claim in lieu of a reduced sentence."

"You're not letting him go, are you?" Erich asked. Lukas frowned at him for acting so bold, but the prince did not seem to take offense.

"There will be consequences. He will not be executed, if that's what you mean, but his political influence is gone, and as word spreads of his villainy, his connections will be severed. No one will want to associate with a traitor. His business assets are forfeit, but that won't amount to much, if anything."

"How can that be? I thought he was extremely wealthy," Anika said.

"Part of an elaborate web of lies, apparently. Lord Leuthold was actually on the brink of bankruptcy. This was his one chance to keep his house solvent. That's why he risked so much."

"Idiot," Ilse muttered. "The one spy we captured is dead, so we have no confirmation who hired him. Worse, that Spitter escaped." She clenched her fists as she spoke, looking like she was eager to finish the meeting to resume the hunt.

"How did she manage that?" Anika asked.

"With help," Lukas said. "No one actually saw the other conspirators, but she escaped Ilse with the help of fire and earth."

Anika exchanged surprised looks with Erich. She hadn't heard about that part. She'd managed to get thoroughly lost in the formal gardens until other searchers had finally shown her the way out.

It was unusual to risk so many senior Petralists on a single mission, but if so many were committed, why not risk a second assault against the palace?

Ilse said, "The spies were exceptionally well trained and crafty. I've inquired of my intelligence contacts, but no one seems to know anything about a young Sehrazad Spitter named Nuzha."

"If she wasn't Obrioner, do you think she was Mhortair?" Erich asked.

The very thought sent a shiver down Anika's spine. The deadly Mhortair assassins could have pulled off such a daring escape. The woman had been arrogant enough to be part of that shadowy group.

"It's possible," Prince Theodor admitted. "I summoned Lady Briet to my office this morning to confront her with the facts. Never to my knowledge have the Arishat League attempted action with the Mhortair during a peace summit.

Such an egregious breach of etiquette is just short of a declaration of war."

"She'd never admit it, not when their agent escaped," Erich said.

"She didn't, but she was deeply embarrassed. She even offered assistance from the Althing treasury in repairing the damage done to Reizend. It's clear all sides know they were involved, but we lack the facts to make a public accusation."

"So the summit is canceled?" Anika asked, feeling relieved. She would welcome a break from her duties.

Prince Theodor chuckled. "On the contrary, Lord Ramwold is already eagerly negotiating terms for a far more favorable treaty than anything our Arishat guests ever expected to agree to. They really have no choice if they wish to avoid escalating hostilities at a time when Obrion is flexing their strength. They took a terrible gamble and now they have to pay the price for failure."

"What to do about you, though?" the prince added to Anika, giving her a thoughtful look. "I'm afraid I must relieve you of your current duties with the battle maidens as well as your position with the florist guild."

Anika's heart sank, and she struggled to think of a way to apologize better. Hadn't the prince just said he didn't blame her? Why choose to punish her too?

She started to stammer another apology, but Erich squeezed her arm and said, "Will you be quiet? Just once? For one minute?"

The others were grinning, including Prince Theodor, so Anika bit her tongue, silently vowing to punch Erich over the house during their next training session.

"I see only two possible options," the prince continued, glancing at Lukas and Ilse. "Have you resolved your impasse?"

Lukas muttered, "I still think she'd make an excellent Crusher."

Isle gave him a charming smile. "But my husband has chosen the path of wisdom."

The prince grinned. "I suspected he would. Good man. I guess that settles it."

"Settles what?" Anika dared ask.

Ilse rose and said, "Starting tomorrow, you report to me."

"Really?" Anika gasped, shocked and thrilled so that the word squeaked a bit as she tried to force it out.

Captain Ilse nodded. "As of today, you have joined an elite, clandestine company, dedicated to the defense of Granadure against all enemies. Our missions are those that cannot be undertaken openly by the crown, but which must be done. We risk our lives to accomplish those critical assignments vital to our continued freedom from all foreign incursion."

Anika listened with rapt excitement. She was in! She'd done it!

"Are you willing to accept my command without question, no matter what I order you to do?" Ilse asked.

Anika nodded quickly. "Yes!"

"Will you trust that I act in the best interest of our nation, and that any sacrifices we make are for the greater good?"

"Yes!"

Ilse grinned and extended her hand. "Then welcome aboard."

## 20

## DATES ALL AROUND

The next afternoon, Anika sat on a simple, wooden chair in a mostly-bare room, across a rickety, scarred old table from Sophie. A slender, glass vase stood on the table, with one of the precious lebhaft roses inside, lending an air of authenticity to the scene. Sophie sat on a three-legged stool, grinning widely as she raised a chipped, wooden tankard of most juice.

"Success to the guild," Sophie said as Anika clinked mugs with her.

"Success to the guild," Anika repeated, then savored a long sip.

They were enjoying a celebratory toast in the florist guild's newly acquired quarters, which would double as Sophie's apartment. Located above a successful bakery shop in a prosperous section of Golm, it would work splendidly once Sophie acquired some furniture.

In addition to the chairs and table, which they'd found in a closet, Sophie had only her bedroll and clothes. Anika had been surprised to learn that she'd been renting a closet-sized room in a dilapidated boarding house, and that had been a big step up from her last residence.

As they savored their drinks, Sophie kept glancing around, as if trying to convince herself that her newfound success was really happening.

"Are you ready?" Anika asked.

Sophie beamed and nodded. "After surviving that summit, I'm ready for anything."

"Good. The girls need a strong leader to build on what we started."

"I still can't believe you're leaving all this behind," Sophie said.

Anika shook her head slowly. Her time as a florist would always be one of her most cherished memories, and she'd be lying to herself if she didn't admit she would indeed miss some aspects of that life.

"I love what we accomplished together, but I have a unique opportunity to fight for our country. I can't walk away from that duty either."

Sophie nodded. "I understand, I think. But you'll always be a part of the guild."

"Good, because the guild is going to owe me a lot of money," Anika said as she pulled from a pocket a rolled parchment and handed it to Sophie.

Sophie took it eagerly. "The perfume?"

"Yes. This is the flower combination I think will best work with the dunkelrot to produce the best recipe. I included the names and addresses of the women who bid for the recipe, as well as the highest bid they offered."

Sophie scanned the list. "Interesting choices. I think this could work exceptionally well." When she looked at the high bid, she whistled softly, her eyes wide. "So much, and just on the bouquet?"

"They're eager for a sample. If we can get them one

soon, I bet we can more than double that number. You know a perfumist you trust?"

Sophie nodded again. "I do. We'll do some testing and try some variations, but I think we could have initial samples ready within a month."

"Excellent. While you're negotiating, mention that Prince Theodor expressed interest in purchasing the first bottle as a gift for his wife."

Sophie gasped. "Are you serious?"

"Absolutely. Captain Ilse mentioned the perfume venture, and he said, 'If you can squeeze perfume from flowers half as well as you throw shoes, I have no doubt you'll produce the best perfume on the market'."

Sophie giggled. "He didn't."

"He did." Anika smiled at the memory. The prince had also insisted on Lady Katrin paying Anika a hefty bonus for the wonderful success of the florist guild. That money would be more than enough to set up the guild until the perfume payments began, even after Anika took her percentage.

"That'll double the highest bid again, at least," Sophie said, rubbing her hands together in anticipation. "What percentage will you let the guild keep?"

"Split it fifty-fifty," Anika said.

Sophie gaped. "Are you sure? It's your recipe."

"But you and the girls will be doing the work managing it. Send my share to my parents. I'll be moving around a lot." Knowing that her parents would enjoy such an elevated income filled Anika with peace. She could dedicate herself to service and adventure in Ilse's company without worrying for her parents.

"Done," Sophie declared, holding out her hand.

Anika took it and they shook firmly. "I expect to hear great things about the guild."

"So do I," Sophie chuckled. "We've already got orders pouring in. Word of our success at the summit is fueling an incredible demand for guild arrangements."

"Good. The girls did great work. I'm glad they'll have plenty of projects."

"Almost too many. I've already talked with Lulu about taking on the role as our new florist recruiter. We'll need apprentices to take over street corner sales while the more experience florists focus on higher-value orders."

"Good idea."

Sophie leaned back, finished her drink, then sighed. "The one challenge I wasn't expecting, but which might prove significant in the near future is turnover of florists due to marriage."

"Really?" Anika hadn't thought about that, but it made sense. When a florist wed, she might not have the same amount of time to dedicate to her job.

Sophie chuckled, nodding. "Indeed. Quite a few of us have received promising attention from staff or workmen they met through the summit."

"You too?" Anika asked. Sophie was skilled at attracting the attention of men, but Anika hadn't noticed her pay any particular attention to anyone during the summit. Her behavior and focus had remained impeccable.

Sophie flashed a mischievous smile. "I've been approached by no less than half a dozen potential suitors."

"Any worthy ones?"

"One, at least. He's a soldier in the prince's guard. He's very handsome, and I think I like him," Sophie said, her smile softening.

Anika was happy for her, and she knew Sophie would not sell her affection without proving the worth of any suitor she accepted.

"And then there's Maud," Sophie continued. "She's

already being courted by a baker's apprentice. He serves in the bakery downstairs, and would make a wonderful husband for her."

That was great news, but Anika worried Maud wouldn't show the proper restraint. "Have you appointed anyone over virtue-defense training?"

Sophie laughed. "I knew you'd bring that up."

"Of course. A girl needs to make her man prove himself."

"We can't all wrestle like you."

"But there are steps that should be taken anyway," Anika insisted.

Sophie raised a calming hand. "I know, and I agree. I'm watching over Maud, and I'll figure out the best way to counsel the girls and provide any coaching they require."

"Good." Anika wanted the girls to find happy relationships, and to enjoy healthy ones for the rest of their lives.

"Have you thrown that handsome sergeant out a window yet?" Sophie asked in a teasing tone.

Anika leaned back, met her gaze, and grinned. "I've accepted his invitation to dinner tonight. Then we'll see if he's got strong hands or not."

She hoped he did. Where else would she find a man worthy to stand with her?

<<<<>>>>

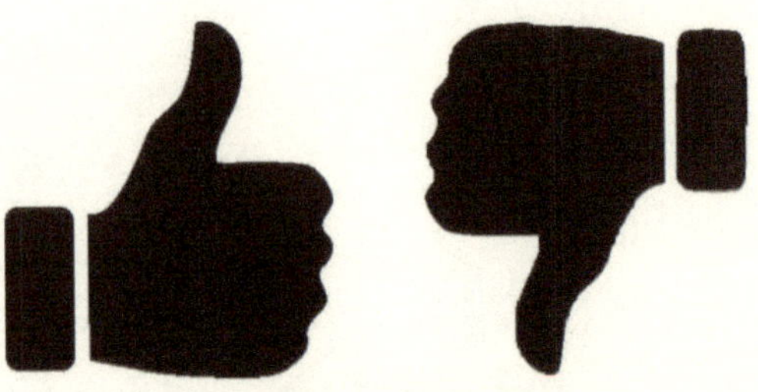

## Thumbs Up?
## Or Thumbs down?

How did you like the book?

Are you willing to take 5 seconds and share it with the world? Now, while it's still fresh?

Reviews help more than you imagine. How many times have you looked at reviews of books or products before buying?

If you've never posted a review before, it's super simple. Just two steps:

•Rate the book 1-5 stars. Be honest. Be generous.
•Write a short review. One or two sentences is plenty.

What goes in those sentences? Here are a few suggestions:
•Your feelings about the book.
•Something you loved about it. (no spoilers please!)
•The fact that you couldn't put the book down all night.
•Your favorite line of Sentry speak.
•Who is your favorite character?
•If you were a Petralist, what affinity would you most love to have?

Just pick one suggestion, or come up with your own. It's that simple.

And just like that, you really help me out, and help other readers considering buying this story.

To post a review on Amazon: http://smarturl.it/yv37jy

Thanks!

Frank

Do you want exclusive content?
First notification of new covers, new maps, and upcoming events?
Exclusive opportunities to submit your ideas and suggestions for future stories?

# Join the Reader's Group!

To join: http://smarturl.it/4u6hmm

I send emails to the group on a regular (but not annoying) basis.

I hope you'll join the team. I look forward to your input.

Frank

# PETRALIST STONES

*Three for the masses*
*Two for the many*
*Four for the privileged few*

## IGNEOUS

Basalt
Speed, agility
Tapped: Powder
through the skin
Obrion: Strider
Granadure: Wingrunner

Granite
Strength, summoning
Tapped: Powder
through the skin
Obrion: Boulder or
Fast Roller
Granadure: Rumbler

Obsidian
Magnifies innate abilities
Tapped: Powder through the skin
Obrion: Blade
Granadure: Allcarver
Sedimentary

# Sedimentary

Limestone
Light
Tapped: Held or worn
Obrion: Solas
Granadure: Solas

Sandstone
Healing
Tapped: Held or worn
Obrion: Healer
Granadure: Healer

# Metamorphic

Marble
Fire
Tapped: Under the Tongue
Obrion: Firetongue
Granadure: Flameweaver

Slate
Earth
Tapped: Soles of feet
Obrion: Sentry
Granadure: Sapper

Quartzite
Air, Senses
Tapped: Placed in Mouth
Obrion: Pathfinder
Granadure: Longseer

Soapstone
Water
Tapped: Powder swallowed
with water
Obrion: Spitter
Granadure: Water Moccasin

# AUTHOR'S NOTE

This is the second Origins story in the Petralist world, and like *When Torcs Fly*, it's so fun to dive into the back story of beloved side characters. The idea for *Game of Garlands* came up in one of our Fast Rollers team meetings. It's fun to pick a character then ask, "What's the craziest thing we could have them deal with?"

In the main series, Anika is super scary, and we all secretly salute Captain Rory for being so insane to want to court her. But in this story, it was so fun to explore how she got started, how she dealt with her own fears, and how she found her place. She's a terrifying fighter, but that's not the only thing that defines her. I hope you enjoyed reading it as much as I enjoyed writing it.

Please send me your thoughts regarding which character to next write an Origins story for. You can send your ideas via my website: www.frankmorin.org, or through the Facebook fan group: https://www.facebook.com/groups/2325447721059132

As always, I love to get your feedback and hear what

AUTHOR'S NOTE

you love best about the series, as well as your ideas for other things we should do in the Petralist world.

Thank you for believing!

Frank

# ACKNOWLEDGMENTS

Such a fun book! And as always, many people helped bring it to life. Here are just a few I need to thank:

- My local Fast Rollers team for helping brainstorm the idea
- Judy Samuelson from Judy's Florist for reading the drafts from an expert's point of view to help it seem like I actually know something about flowers. (I know my wife loves them!)
- Joshua Essoe for another brilliant edit, as usual.
- And for the gorgeous cover, I drew upon the impressive skills of Christian Bentulan. Sweet work!
- As always, thanks to my lovely wife Jenny for her insightful comments and deft editing assistance. You never cease to amaze me.
- And to my kids whose never-ending enthusiasm helps more than they know. Our laughter-fests fuel the life of these Petralist stories.

And finally, THANK YOU to my amazing fans. Your enthusiastic support keeps me motivated to get these stories to you. You're amazing, and knowing you're eager for another book helps me dig deep to produce the very best stories for you.

ALSO BY FRANK MORIN

THE PETRALIST SERIES

*Set in Stone* — Book One

*A Stone's Throw* — Book Two

*No Stone Unturned* — Book Three

*Affinity for War* — Book Four

*The Queen's Quarry* — Book Five

OTHER PETRALIST STORIES

*When Torcs Fly* — Tomas and Cameron prequel

*Game of Garlands* — Anika prequel (you're reading it!)

THE FACETAKERS SERIES

*Face Lift* — Prequel short story

*Saving Face* — Prequel

*Memory Hunter* — Book One

*Rune Warrior* — Book Two

*Aeon Champion* — Book Three (coming soon!)

SHORT STORIES

*Odin's Eye* — Part of *A Game of Horns: A Red Unicorn Anthology*

*Only Logical*—Part of *Unseen: United! Box Set Anthology* to raise funds to fight plagiarism

*The Essence*—Part of *Dragon Writers: An Anthology*

# ABOUT THE AUTHOR

Frank Morin is an avid storyteller and story consumer. When not writing or trying to keep up with his active family, he's often found hiking, camping, Scuba diving, or enjoying other outdoor activities.

Frank writes all types of fantasy, from his exciting Facetakers time-travel fantasy thrillers, to these popular Petralist novels, and more. Check his website for updates and to sign up for his newsletter to receive the latest on all his releases, scheduled events, and insider information:

www.frankmorin.org.

Or you can follow him on Twitter: @MorinWrites

Or like his Facebook page: www.facebook.com/author-frankmorin

Frank lives in Oregon with his family, who are his most enthusiastic fans and his most brutal critics. In their home, storytelling is a cherished family tradition that keeps magic alive.

www.ingramcontent.com/pod-product-compliance
Lightning Source LLC
Chambersburg PA
CBHW050524190726
48284CB00003B/934